"On the surface, an enchanting read about a 7th grade girl and her impossibly intelligent parrot (and no, none of my parrots have achieved quite as much as the fictional Ludwig). But the book is much more, showing how the protagonist deals with mental bullying, cheating by other students, friendship, and being part of a family headed by a single mother. Joanne Levy has succeeded again!"

—*Irene M. Pepperberg, PhD, president of The Alex Foundation and adjunct research professor at Boston University*

Praise for other books by Joanne Levy

"A heartfelt and expertly written tale of loss, family, and friendship that will have readers blinking back their tears… Beautiful and sincere."

—*Kirkus Reviews, starred review, on Sorry For Your Loss*

"This highly discussable novel navigates complex feelings gracefully…Despite the heavy topics this unique novel addresses, it features humor and warmth and characters young readers will care about."

—*School Library Journal, on Sorry For Your Loss*

"Levy presents a realistic, gutsy, problemsolving youth navigating difficult situations with the love and support of community, friends, and family."

—*Booklist, on The Book of Elsie*

BIRD BRAIN

Joanne Levy

ORCA BOOK PUBLISHERS

Text copyright © Joanne Levy 2024

Published in Canada and the United States in 2024 by Orca Book Publishers.
orcabook.com

All rights are reserved, including those for text and data mining, AI training and
similar technologies. No part of this publication may be reproduced or transmitted
in any form or by any means, electronic or mechanical, including photocopying,
recording or by any information storage and retrieval system now known or to be
invented, without permission in writing from the publisher.

Library and Archives Canada Cataloguing in Publication
Title: Bird brain / Joanne Levy.
Names: Levy, Joanne, author.
Identifiers: Canadiana (print) 20230184979 | Canadiana (ebook) 20230185010 |
ISBN 9781459837713 (softcover) | ISBN 9781459837720 (PDF) |
ISBN 9781459837737 (EPUB)
Classification: LCC PS8623.E9592 B57 2024 | DDC jC813/.6—dc23

Library of Congress Control Number: 2023933535

Summary: Even though Arden always wanted a pet, taking care of
her uncle's parrot, Ludwig, was NOT what she had in mind. But as
Arden gets to know Ludwig, she realizes he is not only incredibly
smart but loyal—and the best pet she could have asked for.

Orca Book Publishers is committed to reducing the consumption
of nonrenewable resources in the production of our books. We make
every effort to use materials that support a sustainable future.

Orca Book Publishers gratefully acknowledges the support for its
publishing programs provided by the following agencies: the Government of
Canada, the Canada Council for the Arts and the Province of British Columbia
through the BC Arts Council and the Book Publishing Tax Credit.

Cover design by Rachel Page
Cover artwork and author and parrot bio illustrations by Amy Qi
Interior design by Ella Collier
Edited by Sarah Howden

Printed and bound in Canada.

27 26 25 24 • 1 2 3 4

This book is dedicated to Dr. Irene Pepperberg and Alex (in memoriam), who inspired me to learn more about the fascinating world of African Greys and even add one to my family.

ONE

When my uncle Eli arrived for dinner on that Sunday, I could tell he was distracted the second I opened the door. Well, more distracted than usual—he was the kind of guy who seemed to *always* have a thousand things on his mind.

"Hiya, Ardi," he said like he always did, bending down to give me a hug. But there was something different about him. His hair was more messed up than normal, and while he was smiling, his eyes weren't crinkled up at the corners. Like he had gotten some bad news or maybe he was feeling sick. Something was off, and I wanted to know what.

He was the one who had taught me that the key to being a good scientist was to develop what he called critical thinking skills and to question everything.

"Hi, Uncle Eli," I said as he shrugged out of his jacket and hung it up in the tiny hall closet, shoving aside our coats to make room. Mom kept saying we needed to move out of our crowded condo, and I wouldn't mind too much if we did—then

I wouldn't have to share a room with my fourteen-year-old sister, Chloe, anymore. But Mom hadn't told us to start packing yet, so who knew when or if it would ever happen.

"Everything okay?" I asked.

"Sure, of course. Why?" He cocked his head to the side. "Did your mom say something?"

Now I was *really* suspicious.

He was hiding something.

"No, Mom didn't say anything. Should she have?" I asked, looking at him sideways. "I'm questioning everything, just like you taught me."

His smile *did* crinkle his eyes then, and he ruffled my hair before saying, "Clever girl. All will be revealed in good time." Then, without explaining what *that* meant, he changed the subject, looking right into my eyes and asking in a low voice, "How were things this week?"

I glanced around to make sure there was no one else close, since what he was asking about was a secret I'd told only to him. "The same."

He shook his head. "What did she do this time?"

I took a breath, fighting the tightening in my throat that happened every time I thought about Marni. "She called me a nerd."

Uncle Eli frowned. "There are worse things she could call you. I mean, *I'm* a nerd. It's not much of an insult."

With the way he worked all the time, talked about science stuff, had messy hair and wore dark-rimmed glasses and bow ties, he *was* a nerd. But he totally owned it and was like the coolest nerd ever. He was right that the word on its own wasn't an insult, especially if it meant I was like him. Except he wasn't in seventh grade with Marni Olsen. Who had only said it to be mean.

"I know," I said. "It's…the *way* she said it."

He looked at me for a long moment and then shut the closet door. He had to stuff the coats in so it would latch. He turned back to me and said, "Ignore her. Words are just that—words."

"I guess," I said. But ignoring her wasn't so easy. And words felt like a lot more than simply a bunch of letters put together when Marni hurled them at me like rocks.

Uncle Eli put his big hand on my shoulder, looking at me intently all of a sudden. "She hasn't hurt you physically, has she?"

"No," I said, shaking my head. "She's just the queen of saying mean things."

He nodded, looking relieved. "Okay. But don't forget—"

I interrupted. "I know. Anything physical, and I tell a teacher or Mom right away."

He gave my shoulder a squeeze.

"Thanks, Uncle Eli," I said, my voice squeaky because my throat had gotten tight again. Of course if Marni hit me or tripped me, I'd say something. But the things she *said* hurt too. Just in ways no one could see. Didn't that matter?

"C'mon." He turned us toward the kitchen. "It smells great in here," he said loudly.

I followed him and watched as he gave Mom a kiss on the cheek. "What are we having?" he asked. "Something to keep the vampires away, I presume, based on what smells like the eighty-four cloves of garlic you must have used."

Mom laughed. "Lasagna, salad and garlic bread. And I only used eighty-*three* cloves, but nice try." Then she turned to me and said, "Go wash up. Get your brother and sister too."

I was just outside the kitchen when I heard my uncle say, "You haven't told her?"

"No. I thought I'd leave that pleasure for you," Mom said. "You know how long she's wanted a pet. With how small this place is, it didn't make sense, but…" She trailed off.

But what? A pet was the one thing I wanted more than anything. Maybe even more than I wanted to win the school Science Bowl.

I strained my ears to hear more, but then my mother's head popped around the corner, scaring me and making me squeak.

Her eyebrows went up high on her forehead. "Hands, siblings, now," was all she said, but it was enough.

As I went down the hall, I couldn't help but wonder: Was I getting a pet? Was that what Uncle Eli had been thinking about when he'd first come in, making him seem distracted? If so, why did he seem…not exactly happy about it? Also, why *now*? It wasn't anywhere near Hanukkah or my birthday, and my bat mitzvah was over a year away. What was going on?

Time to employ the scientific method. Step one—observe.

I poked my head into my brother's room to tell him to wash up for dinner. Brandon was sitting on his bed, wearing his headphones. He noticed me and looked up as he pulled them off.

"What?" he said. I barely noticed when he was rude anymore. Chloe—my sister and his twin—was *way* ruder, and I had to share a room with her.

"Dinner," I said. And then, "Have you observed anything strange around here?"

"Strange like what?"

I shrugged. "I don't know. Like preparations for something?" I didn't want to be specific just yet, like mentioning pet food, a litter box, cedar shavings, or leashes and collars, just in case.

But having a pet meant supplies. I had learned all about these things—I'd been researching pets for years, checking out almost every book about puppies, kittens and pocket pets (bunnies, hamsters, guinea pigs) from the library. *No one* was more prepared for a new pet than me.

Brandon frowned. "The only strange thing I've noticed around here is you," he said as he closed his laptop and scooted off his bed.

I rolled my eyes and went to tell my sister it was time for dinner, but she was already in the bathroom, washing her hands.

I pumped some soap into my palm from the dispenser. "Have you noticed anything weird around here?" I asked.

She looked at me in the mirror. "You mean besides you?"

Twins. Sometimes I was sure they shared a brain. "Ha ha," I said, not really laughing. "Hilarious."

She wrinkled her nose in disgust. "You know what's really weird? That whatever-it-is you have growing in our bedroom."

"Uh, it's a mold garden," I reminded her. "A science experiment."

"It's gross," she said. "And it stinks."

She wasn't wrong. But sometimes scientific research could be messy. And smelly. And kind of gross. Still, it was for science. And I had to deal with her taking up most of the closet and with her stinky soccer shoes, which always seemed to find their way under my bed.

"Can we get back to my question, please?" I asked.

Chloe sighed and moved aside when I bumped her with my hip so I could wash my hands. "Weird like what?"

"I don't know," I said, running my hands under the warm water, making lots of bubbles.

"Arden," Chloe said. "What's going on?"

I couldn't contain my excitement anymore. I glanced over my shoulder to make sure we were alone and then whispered, "I think we're finally getting a pet!"

She tsked. Not the excited response I would have expected. "No we're not."

"Yes," I said. "I just heard Mom talking to Uncle Eli."

Chloe finished drying her hands on the towel and then crossed her arms. "Telling him what?" she asked suspiciously.

"That I've wanted a pet forever and that he is going to tell me…something." As I squished bubbles between my fingers, careful to follow proper handwashing procedure, I wondered what my pet would be and what I would name it.

Chloe handed me the towel after I turned off the faucet. "We're not getting a pet. This place is too small for a pet—there's nowhere to put a litter box, and there's no way Mr. Thompson next door would put up with a dog barking."

"Maybe a rabbit," I said. "Rabbits are really quiet."

"And put its cage where?"

"A hamster?" I suggested, even though I'd begun to worry that maybe she was right.

Chloe shook her head. "No way. Our room is small enough as it is. I'm not having a smelly *rodent* in there. Your"—she made air quotes—"*mold garden* is bad enough. Face it, Arden, you heard wrong."

I knew I hadn't, but something was up. The suspense was going to kill me!

"Maybe we're moving," I said, but she just shook her head again.

"No—Mom just ordered that new sofa for the living room. She wouldn't have done that if we were moving. Or getting a pet that would mess it up."

That made sense, but—oh no. Were they going to give me one of those fake Purr-bots? I'd told Mom when she suggested it just before my last birthday that I wasn't interested in anything but the real thing. I mean, who wants a toy robot cat? But maybe Uncle Eli had bought me one anyway.

If that was what this was about, I was going to be *so* disappointed. Worse, I'd have to fake being happy about it so I wouldn't hurt his feelings.

"Kids!" Mom hollered from down the hall. "Let's go. Dinner's on the table."

I hung the towel on the rack by the door and flicked the light off as I followed my sister out to the dining room.

Time for step two of the scientific method—ask questions.

TWO

We all sat down at the table, and I'd gotten as far as putting my napkin in my lap before I couldn't stand it even one second longer. Why were they acting like it was just a normal dinner and they *hadn't* been talking about pets?

"So," I said. "What's new with you, Uncle Eli?"

He'd been reaching for the basket of garlic bread, but his arm froze in the air and he looked at me. Then he looked at my mom and lifted an eyebrow. She sighed and nodded.

Ugh! What's the big deal? Just tell me already!

He grabbed the basket and put a piece of bread on his plate before passing it to Chloe. "Funny you should ask, Arden," he said in a weird TV-announcer-type voice. "There *is* something new with me."

Here it comes, I thought. He's decided to make ALL MY DREAMS come true with a real live puppy or kitten. I felt like my insides were going to jump out of my throat.

"Oh?" I asked, trying not to sound like someone who already knew their dreams were about to come true.

"Yes," he said. "I'm actually going on sabbatical." Then he shoved a forkful of lasagna into his mouth.

What? I stared at him for a long time, but he didn't say anything else. No one else did either. I didn't know what *sabbatical* meant, but it didn't include the words *puppy* or *kitten*, so...

Chloe snorted, and when I glanced at her across the table, she had an *I told you so* look on her face. I glared at her for a second and then looked back at my uncle. "What does that mean?" I asked, still hoping *sabbatical* meant some sort of puppy-shopping expedition or something.

"It means I'm taking time away from teaching to go to Guinea in Africa so I can do some research."

I blinked at him as my heart completely sank.

"That sounds cool," Brandon said. "What kind of research?"

Uncle Eli looked surprised at the question and then shrugged. "Just some botany stuff. Tree bark and seed pods from a rare plant that only grows in a small grove on the other side of the world. I've been planning to go for a while and even got all the vaccinations and travel paperwork sorted, but I wasn't completely sure until last week when my funding finally got approved." He shrugged.

"Oh. Okay," Brandon said before he dug into his lasagna, obviously not interested in tree bark and seed pods. He dropped his head, which I knew meant that as he was eating, he was also looking at the phone in his lap while Mom pretended not to notice.

I wasn't interested in tree bark and seed pods either. Except something on my uncle's face told me *he* was. Which was weird.

Because he wasn't a *plant* scientist. He was a zoologist—someone who studies animals. So why would he be going all the way to Africa to study plants?

I was going to ask, but before I got the chance, his face brightened and he looked at me and said, "That's where you come in, Ardi."

"You want to take me to Africa?" I asked.

Chloe snorted again, but I didn't bother glaring at her this time, too confused to take my eyes off my uncle.

But he laughed too. "No. Though I'm sure you'd be a great research assistant. This is about my parrot."

At first I thought he'd said this was about his *parent*. But that didn't make sense since his parents were my grandparents, and they were down in Florida. Then I realized what he'd *really* said. "Parrot? What?"

I looked at my mom, but she just nodded her head toward Uncle Eli. She didn't seem at all surprised, which meant she'd known about this but had never said anything. Why would she keep this from me?

"I have a new parrot in the lab at the college," he said. "Didn't I tell you about him?"

If he had, I'd forgotten or had put it out of my head on purpose because I hated parrots. Well, I hated the one parrot I'd met—Paco, the giant red and green bird that lived at the pet store. He had a sign on his cage saying to keep your hands away from him because he lunged at people who got too close. One time I'd seen him bite a store employee who was just trying to give him fresh water. There'd even been blood! Because of

Paco, I hadn't ever considered a bird as a possible pet. Your pet shouldn't make you bleed.

Uncle Eli reached for another piece of garlic bread before he said, "Anyway, I can't take him with me, so while I'm away, I'd like you to take care of him."

Wait, what?

"I thought you'd be more excited, Arden," my mother said. "All you ever talk about is how you want a pet. This will be a good opportunity for you to show responsibility, since you'll have to feed him and clean his cage every day."

"Yes, but…" There was a huge lump in my throat, so I couldn't say anything else. I wanted a dog that I could take to the park and play fetch with, or a kitten that would purr when it sat on my lap. Or even a squeaky guinea pig with whiskers. Something fluffy and cuddly. Not a robot, and definitely not a bird.

You couldn't cuddle a bird. Birds were mean and terrifying.

I fought tears and looked down at my dinner, no longer hungry.

"He's a lot of fun," Uncle Eli said. "You'll see."

Maybe my uncle didn't really understand what the word *fun* meant. I mean, he pretty much worked seven days a week—what could *he* know about fun?

"Does he talk?" Brandon asked.

Maybe *he* would want to look after a bird.

Uncle Eli frowned. "A little," he said before shoveling more lasagna into his mouth.

"What does he say?" Chloe asked. "Like, what would a bird talk about?"

While Uncle Eli chewed, Mom said, "It's not like that. Birds that talk just repeat what they've heard. They don't understand what they're saying."

"Actually," Uncle Eli said after swallowing, "there has been a lot of research done on birds and language comprehension. It turns out some birds can be taught to identify different colors and foods and even ask for things they want."

"Cool," Brandon said. "Is your bird like that?"

I looked intently at Uncle Eli because I wanted to know too. If I was going to have to look after this bird, it would be a lot better if it could talk.

Except Uncle Eli shook his head. "He makes some noises, like the coffee maker brewing and the phone ringing, and he says a few words, but that's about it."

"I thought you said he talked," Chloe said.

Uncle Eli sighed. "We're…we've been working with him, but he's new to us. It's a different type of research that's, well, it's not going as well as we'd hoped. That's one of the reasons I'm going on sabbatical. I need to do field research."

"Oh," I said, disappointed.

Uncle Eli turned to me, frowning. "I hope that's not a deal-breaker for you. Your mom said you'd be excited about looking after him."

I opened my mouth to tell him I didn't want to look after his bird, but then I glanced at my mother. She was looking at me expectantly, and I thought about her using the word *responsibility*. This felt like a test. One that if I failed might mean I'd *never* get a pet of my own.

I took a deep breath before I pasted a smile on my face and nodded. "I *am* excited, Uncle Eli! I'm sorry if it didn't seem like it. I was just surprised, that's all."

He smiled, looking relieved. "Great. Thank you. That will be a big help to me while I'm gone."

"When do you leave?" I asked.

"A week from tomorrow, but I'll bring him over on Friday so he can settle in before I go. I'll need to show you all the ins and outs of handling and caring for him."

My stomach lurched as I thought about Paco at the pet store. "What do you mean *handling* him? He lives in a cage, doesn't he? I don't want to get bitten."

"You probably won't get bitten," he said. "If you're careful and learn to respect his signals."

"*Probably?*" Mom asked before I got the chance.

He waved her off and started scooping out another big piece of lasagna. Somehow he had no trouble eating, but I traced my fork around my plate, my appetite gone along with all my dreams of getting a puppy or kitten. And of keeping all my blood inside my body. Although I hadn't thought *that* was a dream until just now.

"How long will you be gone for?" Brandon asked.

"About six months," Uncle Eli answered.

"Six *months!*" I exclaimed.

But at least he was leaving behind a scary bird that didn't talk much and *probably* wouldn't bite me. I groaned.

My uncle chuckled. "I know, I know, you're going to miss me terribly."

It was a joke, but when he said it, I realized what six months without him really meant. Of course I would miss him. He was my favorite family member. The one who took me to the zoo or the science center on PD days when Mom had to work. Who called just to talk to me. Who told me I would be a great scientist someday. The one grown-up I told almost everything to because he understood me better than anyone else and really cared. My throat got tight. I took a breath and reached for my glass of water.

"And I'll only be as far away as an email or text, Arden," he said reassuringly. He knew me so well—so much better than anyone else did—that he could see I was upset, which just made it worse. "It'll be fine. You'll see."

Losing my uncle for six months *and* having to look after a bird?

I seriously doubted it was going to be fine.

THREE

After Uncle Eli left with his container of lasagna, I texted my best friend, Cabbage, to tell him I was coming over.

Since Cabbage lived in our building, just down the hall from us, I was allowed to stay out later visiting him than if I had to go outside. So even though it was a school night, Mom said I could go see him for an hour.

I left our condo, not bothering to change out of my slippers to pad down the carpeted hall to his door.

I liked visiting Cabbage not only because he was my best friend but also because he had a cat named Calliope—Callie for short. He didn't seem to appreciate her. He called her old and hairy, saying all she was good for was to sleep all day and spread cat hair everywhere. He was just mad because she didn't seem to like him much, but he still had to clean out her litter box every day. If I had a cat, I wouldn't mind scooping out the litter box. In fact, I'd even had Cabbage show me how and had done it for him a few times. Although when I'd told Mom I knew how to keep a litter box clean, she seemed unimpressed and told me to go wash my hands.

I knocked on Cabbage's door. A moment later the door opened and there stood Mrs. Devi, wearing a big smile like always. "Allô, mon petit chou," she said in her fancy French accent, standing back so I could step past her. "Henri is in the den."

I nodded and thanked her before I followed the noise of the TV to the den. We didn't have a "den"—we just had a regular living room and three bedrooms. But because Cabbage was an only child, his family had extra space in their condo.

Henri was his real name, but ever since I'd heard his mom call him mon petit chou (which was what she called *all* kids), I'd called him Cabbage. *Chou* is French for cabbage.

He didn't mind my calling him Cabbage because he wasn't a big fan of his real name. I thought his name was nice, especially the way his mom said it—*on-ree*, like there was no *H* in it at all, but he'd told me people who weren't French pronounced it wrong, and he hated being called Henry.

As I entered the den, Cabbage looked up at me and paused the video game he was playing. I glanced at the frozen screen and wasn't surprised to see a big knight standing in front of a crowd of gory zombies. *Zombie Slashers* was his favorite game.

"Hey," Cabbage said. "What's going on?"

He knew something had to be up for me to come to his place so late on a Sunday night.

"Where's Callie?" I asked, looking around the room but not seeing the cat anywhere.

Cabbage shrugged. "I don't know. Maybe on my parents' bed, sleeping off her busy day of doing nothing. Why are you here so late? I thought your uncle was over."

I dropped down on the couch beside him. "That's what I wanted to talk to you about."

After I told him the whole story, he said, "Wow. A parrot, huh? That's so cool."

Maybe he hadn't heard *everything* I'd said. "Did you miss the part about how I'll have to clean up bird poop or how birds have giant beaks and I'll be at risk of losing fingers every single day?"

"What kind of parrot is it?" he asked, ignoring my concerns.

I stared at him, because it occurred to me then that I had no idea what kind of parrot it was—I'd just assumed it would be like Paco. I hadn't even asked the bird's name. "I don't know. A parrot. How many kinds could there be?"

He cocked his head. Sometimes Cabbage didn't need to talk at all because I could read his mind. That was one of the things that made us best friends.

"Okay," I said with a sigh, getting his unspoken point. "I know what you're going to say."

His eyebrows went way up on his head as if to say, *Oh, really?*

"That I need to find out what kind of bird I'll be looking after and then go to the library and do my research."

He smiled and nodded. We always did a lot of research—
it was kind of our thing because we both loved learning,
especially sciencey stuff. And we had been doing even more
studying than usual lately, hoping to win the Regional
Science Bowl because the winning team got a free week at
STEM camp.

But the first step was tryouts to get on our school team.
That meant we spent as much time as possible at the library.

Cabbage and I loved going to the library—it was one
of our favorite things to do. While I wanted to be a vet and
almost always did my research on animals (except birds,
obviously), Cabbage wanted to be an astronaut and borrowed
books about physics and stars. It worked out for us, since it
meant we never fought over books to take out.

"We can go tomorrow after school," he said. "I have
basketball after dinner, so I just have to be home by five."

"Cool," I said, getting up off the couch. "I'll ask my uncle
what kind of parrot he is."

"Good plan." Cabbage nodded at me and then picked up
his controller. "See you in the morning."

I said goodbye and then poked my head into the kitchen,
where Mr. and Mrs. Devi were sitting at the table with tiny
mugs in front of them.

"Bonsoir, Monsieur et Madame!" I said to them.

Mr. Devi wasn't French (he was from England and had a
different fancy accent), but he spoke French very well and of
course understood I was saying good night the way Cabbage
had taught me.

Mrs. Devi smiled and waved at me as Mr. Devi began to rise from his chair. "It's okay," I said, holding up my hand, not wanting to trouble them. "I'll see myself out."

I hurried out the door to go back to my own condo. I had an important text to send.

FOUR

"African Grey," I said the next morning when I met Cabbage in the hallway outside my condo.

We met there at seven forty-eight every school day. This gave us more time than we needed to get to school on most mornings, but sometimes the elevators were slow getting to the fifteenth floor (we actually lived on the fourteenth floor, but because thirteen is considered an unlucky number for superstitious people, our building didn't have a thirteenth). On the mornings when the elevator came right away, we had extra time to walk slowly or stop in at the corner store on the way to school, so neither of us minded.

He stared at me like I was nuts. "A frickin' gray what?"

I giggled and shook my head. "No, silly. The parrot. It's called an African Grey—that's the species. The fancy name is…" I paused to pull out my phone so I could read Uncle Eli's message. "*Psittacus timneh.*" I hoped I'd pronounced it right.

"Oh," Cabbage said.

I thought he might have something more to say about that, but he didn't, so I slid my phone back into my pocket and went on. "And his name is Ludwig."

"After Beethoven?" Cabbage pressed the Down button when we got to the elevators. Before he'd decided to become an astronaut, he'd wanted to be a composer, so he'd done a lot of research about music. On some of our walks to school, he'd told me about his favorite ones, so I knew that Ludwig van Beethoven was a guy from two hundred years ago who went deaf but still kept writing music.

"I don't think so," I said, hitching my heavy backpack up on my shoulders. I had a bunch of library books to return, so it was really loaded. "After some philosopher or something. The good news is it's not a giant bird like Paco at the pet store."

"*That* bird is *so* mean!" Cabbage said, his eyes widening. He'd been there the time Paco bit the pet-store employee. Whenever we went to the mall, he came with me to check out the pet shop before we went to the telescope and astronomy store—*his* favorite place.

The last time we'd been at the pet shop, all we'd done was walk past Paco's cage, and the bird had growled and lunged at us.

I shivered, worried again about parrot-sitting. For six whole months!

Uncle Eli had assured me Ludwig wasn't mean like Paco. I trusted my uncle, but I was still pretty scared. He'd always told me that when I was afraid of something, I should research it to know if my fears made sense or if they were based on the unknown.

I didn't have to do research to know my fear of losing my fingers made sense—I was very fond of them. It didn't take a scientist to know losing them would be a bad thing.

"What are *you* doing here?"

I looked up to see Meanie Marni and her sidekick, Shannon Latner, standing at the end of our table. I suddenly wondered the same thing about them. What were *they* doing in the school library?

"None of your business," Cabbage said, not even looking up from his research. He never seemed bothered by Marni, even though she was just as mean to him as she was to me. I wished I could be more like him that way.

"I wasn't talking to you, *Henry*," Marni spat out, glaring at Cabbage even though he wasn't looking at her. After a moment, when she must have realized he was never going to look at her, she turned to me. "I asked you a question, Arden."

My face got hot as she stared at me. Avoiding her eyes, I looked down at the books spread out on the table in front of me. They were all about birds and keeping them as pets, so I thought it was kind of obvious what I was doing. But I didn't want to say anything about getting a bird—especially when Marni had the cutest Labradoodle named Prince at home. She'd totally won the lottery when it came to pets, whereas I was about to get a participant ribbon. The kind everyone knows doesn't mean anything.

Even as my heart raced, I shrugged, trying to make it seem like no big deal and covering up the books with my arm. "Nothing. Just studying for the Science Bowl."

"You're *such* a dork," she said as she rolled her eyes and Shannon snickered. "Studying."

I swallowed hard, telling myself I would not cry.

"She's just jealous," Uncle Eli had said when I'd first told him about Marni. "She's insecure about herself, so trying to tear you down makes her feel better."

But that didn't make much sense when Marni was popular, pretty, had the best dog and even had a boyfriend. What about me could *she* have to be jealous of? My mold garden? Please.

"We're busy," Cabbage said, finally looking up from his book. "Get lost."

Marni stuck out her tongue at him and then glared down at me. "Science Bowl is so boring. Which I guess is why you'll fit right in."

"It's for *smart* people, which is why you *wouldn't* fit right in," Cabbage said. He wasn't normally mean like that, but she *had* started it.

Marni seemed surprised at Cabbage's words. I expected her to say something mean in return, but she just sort of huffed and then said, "I'm smart! Shut up, doofus!"

Cabbage rolled his eyes.

Marni wasn't done. "Anyway, like we'd even want to be in the Science Bowl. Come on, Shannon. I don't know why we're wasting time with them. Let's go," she said, turning away.

"I need to go text Brian Newman, my *boyfriend,* about our date this weekend. Because he's *my boyfriend.*"

"Yeah, boyfriend, got it. Goodbye," Cabbage muttered.

I stifled a laugh. Like anyone at our school *didn't* know Marni had gotten the most popular guy in our class to agree to be her boyfriend. She'd practically put it on the big sign on the school's front lawn. No one was surprised, since she was the second-most-popular girl in our class (after Carly Henderson, but she was already dating Zach Winthrop—an eighth grader).

I sighed in relief as I watched them leave the library. Then I turned toward my friend. "Why do they have to be so mean?"

Cabbage looked at me, his dark eyebrows pulled down into a frown. "Don't let them get to you, Arden. Don't you see? That's what she wants—to make you feel like she's better than you."

He made it seem so simple, but when she was being mean to me, I couldn't *not* let it get to me. Didn't he see that? And then there was that whole thing of wondering if maybe she *was* better than me.

Cabbage looked up at the big clock on the wall. "We should go. Have you decided which ones you want to take home?"

I looked at the books arranged on the table and was tempted to take them all, but I didn't want to lug fifty pounds of books in my backpack. I grabbed the one closest to me— *Parrot Pals.* "I'll take this one for now. I can get more tomorrow."

"Okay," Cabbage said as he gathered up his stuff. "But don't forget we've got the Science Bowl tryouts next week. Don't spend all your time reading only about birds."

I nodded. We were hoping to get on the team together. Between us we knew a lot and were sure that if we made up half of a four-person team, we could kick some serious science-knowledge butt. But we didn't know everything, so we needed to study—harder than we'd ever studied before.

FIVE

I wasn't sure who was anticipating the bird's arrival more, Cabbage or me. But while Cabbage was excited, I was an anxious mess.

It was after school on Friday, and we were sitting at the table in my dining room, waiting. Brandon was in his room with his headphones on, my mom wasn't home yet from work at the dentist's office, and Chloe was out with her friends. That left Cabbage and me to get ready for Ludwig's arrival.

We'd moved the dining table to one end of the room to make space. We had no other spot to put the cage in our already cramped condo, so for the next six months the bird was going to live in our dining room.

But that was okay because, thanks to my research, I knew Ludwig would probably like being near us when we ate. Eating is a group activity, and if he could see other members of his "flock" (us) eating, he would know to eat also. Apparently being part of a group is really important to birds. I'd read that they even tend to adopt people if there are no other birds around.

"Want something to drink?" I asked Cabbage. For, like, the third time.

This time he said yes, so I got up and went into the kitchen to get him a glass of milk.

Except that as I was reaching for the handle on the fridge, there was a thud at the front door. I forgot all about Cabbage's drink and ran to let my uncle in.

I threw open the door to find him standing there with a bulging shopping bag in one hand and a cat carrier in the other. For a moment my heart leapt into my throat as I thought he'd brought me a kitten, but then I realized the bird was in the carrier. I couldn't see him, but the way Uncle Eli was holding the carrier very carefully and keeping it level told me Ludwig was in there.

That's when my heart started thumping even harder.

"Hiya, Ardi," Uncle Eli said, pointing his chin toward the dining room. "Let me get past you so I can put this stuff down."

I was about to close the door when I heard metal clattering, and then someone yelled, "Gah! A little help, please!"

I looked out the doorway to see Uncle Eli's best friend and fellow teacher at his college, Simon, coming down the hall, struggling with what looked like a bunch of big cage parts. I was rushing toward him when he stumbled and dropped everything, making me have to jump out of the way of flying metal. It made the kind of racket I knew was going to bring crabby Mr. Thompson out of his condo, the one next door to ours.

Uh-oh.

"I'll help you," I said, running over to the mess of metal. Cabbage appeared, so I handed him one of the pieces and then another as Simon retrieved the biggest parts.

"Grab that, Arden?" Simon said, nodding toward a shopping bag on the floor. I picked it up, making it crinkle and jangle—all the screws and things for the cage were in there.

Then, like I'd expected (I had a feeling he spent his days peeking out his peephole), Mr. Thompson came out into the hall and scowled at us as we all turned to look at him. He was very old—like two hundred or something—wearing a navy-blue golf shirt and beige pants that were pulled up high on his body. He had long brown-and-gray sideburns that looked very prickly. "What is all that noise?" he demanded as his eyes darted around at what we were carrying. "You're not bringing a wild animal into this building, are you?"

"My apologies, sir," Simon said as he struggled to arrange the metal cage components in his arms—which, of course, just made more noise. "This is awkward to carry. And no, it's just a small bird. No lions or tigers. I promise."

"Sorry, Mr. Thompson," I said, cringing when he huffed at Simon's joke. "We'll be out of the hallway in a minute." I let Simon go ahead of me and watched as he angled the sections of the cage to get them through the door, making me wonder just how large this cage would be once they put it together. I figured it must be pretty big if they couldn't bring it over already assembled.

The bird, to my relief, wasn't anywhere near as big as Paco if he could fit into the cat carrier, but I had serious doubts about the cage fitting in our dining room. Mom was not going to be happy about that, but she'd agreed to it, and it was too late to back out now.

As I thought all these things, Cabbage and I followed Simon inside. Uncle Eli was standing in the hallway and directed us to put the cage parts on the floor in the living room. "We'll set it up where there's more space to work. Once we're done, we can roll it into the dining room," he said.

We set the parts down, and I looked around. "Where is the bird?"

Uncle Eli nodded toward the dining room. "In his carrier until we get the cage set up. He's a bit stressed out, so we'll just leave him to settle down."

"Oh. Okay," I said, worried that a stressed-out bird might be a bitey bird. I'd read that birds—especially smart ones like African Greys—were really sensitive and didn't like change. Moving to a whole new place and meeting all new people was a lot of change.

"How can we help?" I asked, surveying the cage parts on the floor.

"Well, Simon's the engineer, so he's happy to do most of the cage assembly, aren't you?"

Simon lifted an eyebrow at my uncle, but he was smiling. Simon was a couple of years older than Uncle Eli and a very nice guy. And secretly I thought he was quite handsome. Although I needed to not think about that while he was standing in my living room, because it was so embarrassing and made my face get all hot. Thankfully, no one noticed.

Uncle Eli looked around. "Oh, I left the food and toys in the car. How about you two run down and grab them? They're the two bags in the trunk. I parked in the visitor spot near the door."

I nodded and caught the keys he tossed to me. "On it. Come on, Cabbage," I said, happy for the distraction.

By the time we returned with the shopping bags full of supplies, Simon and Uncle Eli were almost done setting up the cage. I'd assumed we'd put the cage on the sideboard, but it had its own legs on wheels. It was taller than me and about as wide as Mom's favorite club chair. We had to push the sideboard over so the cage would fit in the corner.

"Whoa," Cabbage said.

Uncle Eli nodded. "It's a big cage, but that means we can put some great toys inside and he'll still have room to stretch his wings."

Which made me think of something. "What happens if he gets loose?" I asked, my stomach starting to do flips. "Is he going to fly around? How am I supposed to catch him?"

I was going to lose a finger for sure. Ugh!

Uncle Eli shook his head. "His wings are clipped, so he can't fly."

I frowned. While I was relieved that I wouldn't have to chase the bird all over our condo, I didn't like the sound of *clipped wings.* "What do you mean?"

"I'll show you when we take him out of the carrier, but you'll see that his wing feathers are cut so he can't get lift. I have the vet trim them every so often when they grow in." He shook his head at me. "They're like fingernails, and he doesn't feel it, so you don't have to give me that sad face. And you shouldn't have to worry about them growing in before I get back—I just had him done."

"But birds are *supposed* to fly," Cabbage said, saying exactly what I was thinking. *Why would you want a bird that can't fly? Isn't flying what makes birds...birds?*

My uncle nodded. "Yes, in the wild they are meant to fly for sure. But in a home it could be very dangerous. He could fly into or *out* a window or, worse, into a pot on the stove."

I looked over my shoulder toward the dining room. "But doesn't he miss flying?"

Uncle Eli looked at me for a moment and then turned back toward the cage and said, "I don't know. I can't tell you if he misses flying, but you'll see that he is an expert climber. He's also a great dancer."

Cabbage and I exchanged glances. "Dancer?" I said.

Uncle Eli smiled at me over his shoulder. "Yes. He loves dancing when you play music. But let's get this cage set up so he can settle in."

That made sense. "What can we do?" I asked.

Uncle Eli pointed with the screwdriver to the shopping bag I'd brought up. "That one has his food and dishes. Pull out one of the stainless steel bowls and fill it about halfway with water."

"What about me?" Cabbage asked. "What can I do?"

Uncle Eli finished and stood up straight, wiping his hands on his jeans and nodding toward the other bag. "That has all of Ludwig's toys and perches. Why don't you pull out all the perches, including the rope one, and we can start putting them in the cage."

When I returned from the kitchen with the bowl of water, Uncle Eli took it from me and put it into the holder inside the cage, showing me how to open the little access doors to refill the food and water dishes. It was a relief to know I didn't have to shove my whole arm in the cage to do that. Also, there was a tray at the bottom of the cage to catch all the bird poop that would fall through the bars, and I could pull it out from the front without opening the cage.

"Now," my uncle said. "There isn't enough of his food to last you the whole six months, so you'll have to go to the pet store. He also gets a special vitamin supplement, but there *is* enough of that to last."

I opened the shopping bag again and pulled out the sack of what looked like colorful cat-food kibble in different shapes. When I opened it, it smelled fruity and reminded me of Skittles candy.

I wondered if it tasted like it. Not that I was going to try it.

Uncle Eli pulled out another storage bag, which was filled with a powder. "Just mix a teaspoon of this in with his food every day. It's really important, so don't forget."

"Okay," I said. "No problem." I took the food, dish and the powder into the kitchen and got out the measuring spoon. I opened up the bag of powder—which smelled earthy, sort of like a forest after the rain—scooped some out and mixed it into the food.

When I brought it back, Uncle Eli was looking around. "Shoot, I forgot to bring some newspaper to line the tray. Do you have some?"

I shook my head. "Mom reads the newspaper on her laptop."

Uncle Eli sighed.

"Wait," I said. "Does it matter what kind of paper it is?"

"Not really," my uncle said.

"Hold on," I said as I jumped up and jogged to the kitchen. I came back with my last math test, which I'd put up on the fridge because I'd gotten twenty-nine out of thirty on it.

I handed it to my uncle.

"Nice job! But are you sure you want to use this?" he asked, looking from the papers to me. "It'll be garbage once Ludwig's through with it."

"It's okay," I said, shrugging. "Everyone's already seen it." I'd made sure of it.

He ruffled my hair and then pulled the staple out of the pages, arranging them around the tray at the bottom of the cage. "You'll need to go out and buy some newspapers or find some of the free ones at the grocery store to use. You'll want to change them every few days."

"Okay," I said, making sure to pay attention to what he was saying and doing, since I would be Ludwig's caregiver for six months. I'd write everything down in a notebook later, to make sure I didn't forget.

As I watched, Uncle Eli installed the perches, which were all different. One was a braided rope, one looked like an old tree branch, and another was made of stone or concrete—whatever it was, it was really rough. Uncle Eli said it was a pedicure perch that would help keep Ludwig's toenails trimmed, because they could get sharp.

Then I got to pick from the assortment of toys he'd brought over. He said to limit them to two at a time and rotate them every week or two so Ludwig wouldn't get bored. I'd read that birds were great at solving puzzle toys, and playing with things in their cages was important.

I picked a hanging toy with a bunch of colorful wooden pieces and leather knots. The second toy was a plastic puzzle toy with a bell on it. Uncle Eli said I could put peanuts and almonds inside, and Ludwig would have to turn all the pieces to figure out how to get the treats out. He said that would keep him busy and that doing it mimicked his natural urge to forage for food.

It was cool learning so much about bird behavior. Knowing more about what the bird needed and how the things in his cage replicated what his life would have been like in the wild made me feel better about the situation and even a little excited to learn more. Maybe even a little less terrified.

Once everything was set up, we rolled the cage into the dining room and tucked it into the corner. Uncle Eli gave it a once-over and nodded. "Okay, let me grab him."

Nope, still terrified!

SIX

I stood there holding my breath as Uncle Eli opened the door to the carrier, slowly putting his hand inside as he spoke softly to the parrot.

"Okay, Ludwig, we're here at Arden's, and she's going to be looking after you while I'm away. Don't worry, she's going to take very good care of you."

A growl came from inside the carrier. I suddenly thought about Paco, worried that my uncle was about to get—

"Ow!" Uncle Eli muttered without raising his voice. "Ludwig. Come on, what did you do that for?"

"Did he bite you?" I whispered.

Uncle Eli exhaled loudly. "Yes, but he's stressed out. He's usually much better behaved than this." I noticed he hadn't removed his hand from the carrier, nor had he screamed, so the bird must not have bitten him very hard. "Step up, Ludwig."

A moment later my uncle's face softened a little. "That's better," he said and then slowly pulled his arm out of the carrier, the bird perched on his hand. The bird—Ludwig—really wasn't very big. He was about the height of a water bottle. He had silvery-white eyes, and his face was white and lined with gray (of course) feathers. He had little nostrils above his grayish-brown beak, and he looked like he was smiling. But I had a feeling he wasn't very happy at this moment.

"His tail feathers are dark burgundy," I said, keeping my voice soft. "Does that mean he's a Timneh African Grey?"

"Yes, that's exactly right," Uncle Eli said, flashing a smile at me. "You've done your research."

I beamed a smile back at him. "Of course I did. I also learned that there are two types of Greys and that Congo African Greys are larger and have brighter-red tail feathers."

Ludwig had a metal ring around his right ankle, but nothing on his left. I wondered if that was on purpose.

Uncle Eli turned little by little toward the cage and continued speaking in a soothing voice. "Just stay still, everyone, while I get him into the cage."

"Whoa," Cabbage said beside me.

That's when I noticed the blood dribbling down the back of my uncle's hand. I couldn't help the squeak that came out of me. "You're bleeding!" I whispered, somehow managing to stay calm on the outside.

Like he hadn't heard me, Uncle Eli put his hand holding the bird through the open cage door and held it beside the tree-branch perch until Ludwig stepped onto it. Then he pulled his arm out of the cage and closed the door with what sounded like a relieved sigh.

"Uncle Eli!"

"I know." He nodded as he cradled his right hand in his left. "Grab me a paper towel?"

"On it," Cabbage said as he turned toward the kitchen.

"Does it hurt?" I asked—ridiculously, because of course it hurt. He wasn't just bleeding, he was *gushing* blood. But what I really wanted to ask was, *Can you please take that dangerous bird away?* I'd been right to be terrified. Birds were the worst!

"It's not as bad as it looks," he said, though I was sure he was fibbing. Especially when I saw the pinched look on his face. Cabbage came back and handed him several paper towels, which my uncle took and pressed against his hand.

I turned and looked at the bird, whose silver eyes seemed to be on me. Then he started growling again. What a terrible sound to come out of a bird!

"Okay," Uncle Eli said after huffing out a breath, "so maybe not the best first impression, Ludwig, but this is my niece, Arden, and like I said, she's going to be looking after you for the next while."

Not if I have anything to say about it, I thought.

"Does he understand what you're saying?" Cabbage asked. Which was weird because had he not seen all that blood? Oh wait, *he* didn't care about blood—*he* wasn't the one who had to look after the bird for the next six months.

Uncle Eli looked from Ludwig to Cabbage. "Um...I don't think so, but talking to him in calm tones will help him settle down. He's sensitive and takes his cues from me, so if he sees that I'm not panicking, he'll know there's nothing really scary going on."

Right. Nothing really scary, just some regular, everyday carnage. I'd seen Cabbage defeat zombies in his video games who'd come away with less flesh missing.

"But he bit you," I said.

Uncle Eli lifted the paper towel away from his hand. At least he was no longer gushing blood. "He did," he said. "But he was frightened and lashed out because he felt threatened. But if you take your time with him and don't make sudden moves while he's getting to know you, he shouldn't bite you."

Shouldn't.

"Didn't it hurt, though?" Cabbage asked. "I mean, you didn't pull your hand away from him. Didn't that make him madder?"

I looked at my uncle intently, because I wanted to know the answer.

"Actually, the opposite," he said. "When I made it seem like his bite was ineffective and wasn't going to make me take my hand away, he stopped biting. If I *had* pulled my hand away and made a big deal out of it, he would have learned that biting is a good way to get what he wants. Which is the last thing we want to teach him."

I nodded. My throat tightened because I was convinced that this bird was going to be the worst pet ever.

Uncle Eli stepped over to me and put his arm around my shoulder. "It's okay, Ardi. Just keep talking to him, and soon he'll get used to you. You'll be best friends in no time, you'll see."

I glanced at Cabbage. "Yeah, so I already have a best friend, and he almost never bites me."

"She has a point, Eli," Simon said with a laugh. "No one needs friends like that. Why don't we sit down and just talk around Ludwig so he gets used to the room and all of us. Then you can handle him again. The more she sees you handling him, the more comfortable she'll feel doing it herself. What do you say, Arden?"

I nodded. Simon was so nice.

"Good idea," Uncle Eli said. "I meant to type all this up for you, but there's so much I still have to do to prepare for the trip."

I'd planned to write everything down after he left, but it was starting to feel like it was more than I was going to remember. "Let me get my notebook," I said. "I don't want to forget anything."

"Wait," Cabbage said as he pulled his phone out of his pocket. "I'll just film this so we can play it later."

"Perfect," Simon said. "Good thinking."

An hour later, after Cabbage had left to go home for dinner, Mom arrived with two giant brown bags of Chinese takeout.

Brandon must have smelled it, because a second after Mom opened the first bag, he emerged from his room.

Since Simon and Uncle Eli were still there, Mom invited them to stay and eat with us. They were both happy to stick around. And if I wasn't seeing things, it seemed like Simon kept sneaking looks at my mom. My mom, who hadn't been on a date in forever. Maybe if she had a nice, handsome boyfriend, she wouldn't want to work so much.

Potential romance aside, I was relieved he and Uncle Eli had stayed, because even though Cabbage had recorded the instructions, and I'd taken some notes, I still wasn't ready to be left alone with Ludwig.

Uncle Eli must have sensed this, because he said we'd give the bird the night to settle in and he'd return the next day so he could help me with Ludwig's morning routine.

I felt better about that—although that would only get me through Saturday. On Sunday Uncle Eli had to prepare for his trip, and Monday, he was leaving for Guinea. In Africa. Literally half a world away.

As we ate, he told us all about his travel plans and how hard it was to get to the village he was going to. Brandon asked him why he was going all that way just to study tree bark, something I was wondering too.

But Uncle Eli just shrugged and said, "Field research," before he dug into his Shanghai noodles, using his chopsticks to stuff his mouth full.

At the end of dinner, I broke open my fortune cookie, and the little strip of paper said, *You can cage a bird, but you cannot make him sing.* I looked over at Ludwig. I didn't care if he sang, as long as he didn't bite off any of my fingers.

Ugh. It was going to be a very long six months.

SEVEN

*EEEEEEEEEEEEEEEEEEEEEEEEEEEEEEEEEEEEEEEE
EEEEEEEEEEEE!!!*

"Mrrrrwhaaaaa?" Chloe blurted, bolting up in her bed as I did the same. "What *is* that?"

"Fire alarm!" I shouted, throwing back my covers and jumping out of bed, my heart pounding hard in my chest under my STEM GIRLS pajamas. "Come on!"

We joined Mom and Brandon in the hall, everyone wide-eyed and confused.

"Okay, kids, just like we practi—" Mom broke off because the alarm had suddenly stopped. We all looked at each other.

"Ugh, false alarm," Chloe said.

Then the alarm started again!

"What the…?" Mom said as she began to herd us down the hall again.

"Wait a minute," Brandon said crabbily. He turned and started toward the bright dining room. I'd left the light on so

Ludwig wouldn't have to spend his first night in his new home in the dark.

"I think it's coming from in there," Mom said.

Suddenly the alarm stopped again. We all froze.

"What is going on?" Chloe whined.

EEEEEEEEEEEEEEEEEEEEEEE! and then we heard *Gurglegurglegurgle…shhhhhhhhhh.*

Brandon's eyes went wide. "It's the bird."

"EEEEEEEEEEEEEEEE!"

I slapped my hands over my ears. It was SO LOUD.

"What is it doing?" Mom said over the noise, pressing her fingers to her forehead like she did when she had a migraine.

Then the pounding on the front door started. That was definitely *not* the bird.

Knowing exactly who was at the door, I went the other way, toward the dining room and Ludwig's cage. As soon as I rounded the corner, the fire alarm stopped again. Thank goodness.

I heard Mom open the front door and start apologizing to Mr. Thompson, assuring him it was a false alarm and we had everything under control. But we didn't. Not even a little.

I looked at the bird, who was sitting on his rope perch, staring back at me. He seemed so innocent, sitting there. Not even that big a creature, really. But between Uncle Eli's flesh wound and what would now forever be known as the Three a.m. Ludwig Alarm of Death, I knew better than to underestimate him.

"What was that for?" I asked him.

He just looked at me.

"Not so noisy now, are you?" I said, leaning toward the cage but keeping my hands safely clasped behind my back.

Ludwig cocked his head and stared at me with his right eye. He seemed to be very interested in what I was saying. I wondered if he understood anything. Did he know his name? Who Uncle Eli was? Who *I* was?

"You know," I said to him, "Uncle Eli said we could be best friends, but you're not making it very easy." I couldn't help but think that a puppy or kitten wouldn't have woken up the whole building in the middle of the night.

Ludwig blinked unapologetically.

I sighed and then yawned.

Ludwig yawned, too, his upper beak stretching away from his lower one. Or it was what I *thought* was a yawn. Did birds yawn? If that *was* a yawn, it meant he had caught *my* yawn. Which meant he was paying attention to me.

Hmmm.

"Come on, Arden," Mom said from the doorway, startling me. "Back to bed."

I nodded, tired now that the terror had worn off.

Mom turned out the dining-room light this time. "Do you think we should leave it on?" I asked.

"No," Mom said. "Maybe that was the problem. Maybe if it's dark, he'll just go to sleep."

"But won't he be afraid? Being in a strange place, I mean?" I asked, worried that if he spent the whole night anxious and afraid, he'd be even more bitey in the morning.

"I'm sure he'll be fine," Mom said, sounding sleepy and a little bitey herself. "It's bad enough that Mr. Thompson is upset about *one* interruption. The last thing we need is another."

"Okay," I said and turned toward the cage, seeing only the tiny shimmer that was Ludwig's silver eye staring back at me. "Goodnight, Ludwig," I whispered.

In the morning I woke up and looked at the clock, relieved that we'd made it through the night without any more false fire alarms. It was still early, and Uncle Eli wasn't coming over for a while, so I thought I'd get out of bed and see what Ludwig was up to. Maybe I could at least do his food and water so I didn't look like a total fraidy-cat. Fraidy-*bird*?

I slid my feet into my slippers, grabbed my phone off the charger and left my bedroom, closing the door quietly behind me. Chloe likes to sleep really late on the weekend.

After I used the bathroom, I tiptoed down the hallway past Mom's and Brandon's rooms. I didn't want to startle the bird, so I called out a quiet "Good morning, Ludwig" as I turned the corner into the dining room.

While I'd known the cage door was locked, I was still relieved to see he hadn't escaped in the night. He sat on the tree perch, his head turned, one silver eye looking intently at me.

"I hope you had a good night's sleep, Ludwig," I said, feeling silly but remembering that Uncle Eli had said talking would help the bird feel more calm and learn that he could trust me.

Of course, the bird didn't say anything back and just kept staring at me. I hoped he didn't hate me, but there was no way to know what he was thinking. I wasn't about to stick my arm into the cage to find out if he wanted to take a chomp!

"I'm going to give you some fresh food and water," I said in what I hoped was a soothing voice. "So please don't try to bite me." I took a deep breath and kept my eyes on him while I slowly reached for the little access door in front of the food dish. The bowl was almost empty, and that was a good sign—if he was really stressed out, he probably wouldn't eat.

"Just me, you know, getting you some more delicious birdy kibble," I said, almost singing the words. The bird didn't growl or lunge at me as I took the food dish out. I exhaled in relief.

"Thank you for not biting me, Ludwig." I smiled at him so he knew I was *really* pleased about having all my limbs still intact. I put the shiny bowl on the dining-room table and took out the water dish, noticing there were some food pellets in it. They were all soggy and big, looking like fat little sponges floating on top of the water.

"Huh," I said. "I don't know how the food got in there, but let's get you some fresh water."

I glanced at him. He hadn't moved and was still watching me intently. He was probably wondering who the heck I was.

"Oh, so I guess you don't really know who I am," I said, making sure to smile. "I'm Arden Sachs, and your…uh… owner?… is my uncle Eli. I know he told you, but I'm going to be looking after you while he's in Africa for six months. That's a pretty long time, but maybe not to you, since I know you can live for many, many years. This one book I read said some parrots can live over a hundred years!"

Ludwig suddenly squeaked and shook out his feathers. I held my breath, waiting to see what he would do next, but he just looked at me. Maybe he was waiting to see what *I* would do.

"How old are you, Ludwig?"

He didn't answer.

"I don't know why I'm asking," I said, shaking my head. "You don't understand what I'm saying."

But he was looking at me so intently, it really seemed like he was listening.

I stared at him hard. "*Do* you understand what I'm saying?"

He blinked at me silently. Which wasn't a no. But who was I kidding? He was a bird, and I was the only interesting thing in the room. Of course he was watching me.

But I still couldn't shake the feeling that there was more to his little birdy brain than I'd thought before.

With a shrug I took both dishes into the kitchen. As I poured the water and soggy pellets down the sink, I heard— clear as day—a voice from the dining room say, "Thirty-four."

I froze for half a second and then turned back toward the dining room just in time to hear it again.

"Thirty-four! Thirty-four! Thirty-FOUR."

What the what?!

EIGHT

Ludwig didn't say anything else, despite my encouraging (and—let's be honest—begging), but I knew what I'd heard. So when my uncle *finally* showed up nearly an hour later with a tray filled with to-go cups from Mom's favorite café, the Daily Grind, I was nearly bursting with excitement.

"Uncle Eli!" I said as I swung open the front door for him. "Ludwig! He's thirty-four!"

"Hiya, Ardi." My uncle handed me the drinks and then frowned at me as he toed off his shoes, taking his sweet time. "Thirty-four *what*?" he finally asked.

I rolled my eyes. "Thirty-four years old, duh! He told me when I asked how old he is!"

He frowned. But seriously, what else could I have meant? "No," he said. "He's only about ten. The year of his birth…er… *hatch* is actually on his foot band, along with the information about his breeder."

I hadn't exactly gotten close enough to the bird to read a

tiny date on the ring around his ankle, but at least I knew now what it was for.

Still… "Oh," I said, disappointed that Ludwig hadn't been answering my question.

"But if that's not how old he is, what on earth is thirty-four?" I asked Uncle Eli.

He just shrugged. "No idea. Maybe he was saying something else that sounded like thirty-four. He's often not really precise when he's learning something new. Like, maybe he was saying, 'Eli's a bore,' or 'I heard Arden snore.'"

I blew a raspberry. "I don't snore! But that other thing could be true." I said it with a smile so he'd know I was joking.

He grabbed me in a side hug, almost spilling his coffee. "I'm going to miss you."

"Stop talking about it!" I said, feeling my eyes prickle.

"Sorry," he said and cleared his throat. "Anyway, who knows what Ludwig was saying. It could have been anything. Sometimes it's just sounds."

I supposed that made sense, but it was still extremely disappointing since it disproved my theory.

"What's in here?" I asked, nodding at the tray of drinks I'd taken from him.

"Oh, right," he said, shaking his head as though he'd forgotten. Typical. "Coffee for your mom, and hot chocolate for you, Chloe and Brandon."

"Marshmallows?"

"Please," he scolded. "This isn't my first day as best uncle ever."

We went into the kitchen, where Mom was sitting in the booth against the wall. She looked up from her laptop and smiled. "About time you brought that coffee in here," she said with a laugh and a fake scowl. I handed her the cup with the *B* written on the lid because she took her coffee black, which means just plain, without cream or sugar. Gross. I opened up my hot chocolate and took a sip. Delicious.

Uncle Eli delivered Chloe's and Brandon's drinks and then returned to the kitchen. "C'mon," he said and nodded his head toward the dining room. "Let's get him set up for the day."

"I already did his food and water," I said proudly. "And his vitamin powder, of course."

"Did you? That's awesome." He gave me one of those big smiles that made his eyes crinkle. "I knew you were the perfect person to look after him."

"As long as he doesn't bite me," I said, noticing the Band-Aid on his hand.

"He shouldn't," Uncle Eli said. "But I don't want you to be afraid of him. If he thinks he can scare you by biting, he will lunge, and then you might end up having trouble holding him. Not that he's going to be crabby all the time, just if you're asking him to do something he doesn't want to do. He has a very strong personality."

Holding him? Yeah, so that wasn't happening anytime soon.

Uncle Eli patted my arm. "I know it can be scary, and the last thing I want is for you to get bitten, but you need to be confident when you handle him."

I didn't feel very confident. At all. "But Paco has signs on his cage not to get close to him."

"Who's Paco?"

"I told you, remember?" I took another sip of my hot chocolate before I said, "The mean bird at the pet store in the mall. He's why I never wanted a bird."

"Oh, right." Uncle Eli nodded sadly. "That's different. He probably *is* really mean because of years spent in the pet store in a very stressful situation. Definitely stay away from birds like that—he probably gets teased all the time and might feel he has no choice but to bite people to keep them away. Ludwig is different. He really isn't mean. He was just frightened yesterday."

"He didn't growl at me when I gave him food and water," I said proudly. "I talked to him and told him what I was doing."

"See?" Uncle Eli said with a big smile. "He's already getting used to you. You obviously have great instincts when it comes to dealing with him. He might growl at the vacuum cleaner if you're pushing it around his cage—it's very loud and scary to him. But he'll get used to you, and you'll be fine when you go to handle him."

All of a sudden a sound came from the dining room. "Ker-chunk. Beep-beep-beep. Hmmmmmm, hmmmmm, hmmmmm." It wasn't really loud like the fire alarm, but it had obviously come from the bird—which was pretty impressive, since it sounded like a robot noise or something.

"What was *that*?" Mom asked with a laugh.

Uncle Eli smirked. "That was Ludwig imitating me putting my coffee in the microwave to reheat it."

Mom chuckled. "Ah, so you don't just do it around here?"

"Nope," my uncle said. "I'm afraid I do it a lot at work, too, and Ludwig has picked up on it."

"So wait," I said as I closed my eyes, trying to remember the sound I'd just heard. "The ker-chunk…"

"Microwave door," Uncle Eli said. "The beeps are me pressing the buttons, and then the hum of the microwave. I'm surprised he didn't do the ending beep of the cycle. It's funny how you don't notice some sounds until a bird imitates them exactly."

I looked toward the dining room. "Okay, that is hilarious."

Uncle Eli smiled. "Don't be surprised if he makes noises mostly when you're not in the room. He's something of a shy talker. Even when he gets really comfortable, he may be his chattiest when you aren't in view."

"Like the fire alarm?" Mom said dryly. "At three a.m.?"

Uncle Eli's eyes went wide. "Oh no."

I nodded.

He sighed. "There was this one time when I brought him home over a holiday weekend and, well, you all know I'm a bad cook. So when I burned something, he heard the smoke alarm. When I made a big fuss, waving newspaper at the alarm, trying to get the alarm to stop, Ludwig learned it was a fun noise to make that would get lots of attention." Uncle Eli rolled his eyes. "Silly bird! Anyway," he said with an apologetic smile, "I'm really sorry. Hopefully he won't do it again."

I was about to tell him that Mom would ship the bird off to Africa if he got in the habit of doing the fire alarm in the middle of the night when, all of a sudden, Ludwig did the microwave sound again. "Ker-chunk. Beep-beep-beep. Hmmmmmm, hmmmmm, hmmmmm." But then, after about ten seconds, he did a long "beeeeeeeeeep." We all giggled like crazy. Then *he* giggled, making us giggle even more. Uncle Eli gave me a smirky look, as though to say, *See? Isn't he funny?*

So funny. And I thought, All right, maybe Ludwig won't be the worst pet after all.

NINE

We did a bunch of training exercises in which Uncle Eli and I got the bird to step back and forth between our hands. That might sound like a really boring thing to do—to get the bird to just walk from me to him and back, but I have to say it helped me feel much better about handling him. Anyway, it's not like the bird complained about it.

The first time was terrifying, but Ludwig just stepped up and stood on my pointer finger like it was no big deal. He wrapped his little toes around my finger, and it felt weird but not bad at all. He barely weighed anything, and his nails weren't sharp, even though they looked a little scary. He didn't even seem to mind too much that my hand was shaking a little from nerves. Maybe it was like a branch blowing in the wind? Not that there was much wind in my uncle's office in the college, but maybe birds didn't mind if their perches moved a little under them.

"Great job," Uncle Eli said in his calm voice. "Now I'll take him." He put his hand in front of mine but a little higher, then said, "Okay, Ludwig, step up."

And the bird stepped up! We did this for a while, and then Uncle Eli let me give Ludwig an almond as a treat before I returned him to his cage by putting my hand beside his rope perch and letting him step off. A few minutes later I put my hand (confidently) into the cage in front of the bird and said (also confidently), "Step up."

It was by far the scariest thing I'd done all day, but without any fuss or biting, the bird stepped onto my hand!

Mom exhaled loudly, obviously as relieved as I was. But I was more than relieved—I was proud of myself, and I felt a lot more comfortable with Ludwig. Soon I wouldn't have to fake confidence when handling him.

We practiced more and Uncle Eli wrote down a bunch of things about Ludwig that he hadn't thought of before, like his favorite treats (almonds, peanuts, pomegranate seeds) and foods to avoid because they could be poisonous to him (avocados, walnuts, junk food).

"Thank you for coming," I told my uncle when it was time for him to go home and start packing for his long trip. "I feel a lot better now."

"Thank *you* for looking after him," he said, smiling down at me. "I know you'll do a great job and will have a lot of fun. Make sure you keep his cage clean, and change his food and water every day. Oh, and don't forget to give him his vitamins on his food too. That's really important."

I nodded. I took my own vitamins every day, so that would help me remember.

"And let me know how it's going. I may not be able to respond right away if I'm deep in the forest, but that doesn't mean I won't see your messages.

"Now, Ardi," he went on, his tone turning serious as he looked me straight in the eye, "I'm counting on you to look after him. He's not just a pet but also a valuable research subject." He blinked a few times and then said, "And I need to know if he does anything weird."

I tilted my head to the side. "Weird like what?"

"Anything that seems…strange. Or…I don't know…just any behavior that seems out of the ordinary."

Didn't he know that *everything* to do with the bird was strange? That *nothing* was ordinary? I'd never looked after a parrot before! But I promised I would check in with regular status updates.

I could just imagine them. *Bird pooped. Bird beeped. Bird ate pellets. Bird pooped again.*

"Thanks, Ardi," Uncle Eli said. "You'll do a great job—I know it. Six months will be over before we even realize."

I doubted that but didn't say anything. Instead I threw myself into his arms and gave him a big hug because he was leaving for a very long time and I was going to miss him more than anything. He hugged me really tight, and I knew that meant he was going to miss me too.

"Keep me posted about that *other* situation too," he said into my ear so Mom wouldn't hear. "And remember what we talked about."

"I know," I said, my voice squeaky. "I remember."

He pulled out of the hug and gave me a sad look, then said goodbye to my mom (who also got a little teary) and then to Chloe and Brandon, who Mom had hollered for a few minutes earlier. They were sad to see him go, too, but I was going to miss him the most.

"Why's he just staring at us?" Cabbage asked. It was the next day, and we were standing in the dining room in front of Ludwig's cage.

"I don't know," I said. "Maybe because we're staring at him?"

Cabbage looked over at me and then broke into a smile. "Maybe you're right. That's probably rude, huh?"

"He doesn't even know who you are," I said. "I officially introduced myself to him yesterday. Maybe you should too."

Cabbage scratched the back of his neck. "Do you think he understands?"

"No idea." I shrugged. "Can't hurt."

Cabbage nodded and turned back toward the bird. "Hi, Ludwig," he said. "My name's Henri Devi, but Arden here calls me Cabbage, so you'll probably hear that a lot. You can call me either."

"Just not *Henry*," I said. "He hates that."

"Right." Cabbage nodded. "*Not* Henry, please." Then we stood there for a long time, staring again, waiting for a reaction. And waiting. And waiting some more.

Finally, after a very long time, Ludwig did his little feather-fluffing shake.

"What was that?" Cabbage said, full of wonder, like Ludwig had just done something major.

"I'm not sure. He does that sometimes. I think it's to put all his feathers in place."

"Oh," Cabbage said, disappointed.

"Anyway," I said. "Science Bowl tryouts are this week—we should get studying."

"Like you need to remind me?" Cabbage said. But then he looked sort of nervous, which didn't make sense because he's super smart.

"What are you worried about?" I asked. "You're a genius. You're going to go to space someday."

He snorted. "Not exactly."

"What are you talking about?" I said. "You're totally going to crush the tryouts. It's not like these are tryouts for NASA—which I think you'd nail anyway. You're the smartest kid in our class."

"After you, maybe," he said, which was kind of a surprise. I mean, I was smart, but I didn't think I was smarter than Cabbage. We both did well on tests, sometimes even getting the exact same high marks—which made sense since we studied together all the time.

"Whatever," I said. "There are four spots on the team. Both of us will definitely get on, we'll win, and then we'll go to STEM camp."

Cabbage didn't look so sure. "What if they ask us really hard questions in subjects we haven't studied? What if we *don't* make it?"

"We will," I said with the same sort of confidence I'd faked when picking up Ludwig. "You'll see. Who else is trying out?"

"I'm not sure. Probably Charlotte Hughes and Andy Fernandez. Oh, and I think Brian."

"Brian Newman?" I asked, surprised. "Meanie Marni's boyfriend?"

"Yeah. He asked me the other day what he should be studying to prepare."

I have to admit, I was suddenly a little concerned. Despite the fact that he liked Marni, which made me question his intelligence a little, Brian was smart. His trying out might make our getting on the team not a totally sure thing, especially since Charlotte knew almost everything in the life sciences category (which was my second-best category after math, mostly because it included animals) and Andy was almost as good as Cabbage in physical sciences and maybe even better at general science trivia. He wasn't very good with math, though.

Not to mention that there would be other kids trying out (including eighth graders) who we didn't even know about. And, of course, Cabbage was right—if we weren't lucky, and they asked us questions in areas we hadn't studied, we might not make the team.

There was only one way to be sure we would make it. "Come on," I said. "We can study at the dining-room table. I think Ludwig will like it if we're in the room with him. Who knows—maybe he'll learn something."

We both glanced over at the bird, who was still looking intently at us.

"It's weird that he just stares," Cabbage said.

"But it seems like he's really watching us, doesn't it? Like, he's really paying attention to every word?"

"Yeah," Cabbage said. "That makes it even more creepy."

"Whatever." I laughed. "Hey, let's go get some snacks before we start."

We got to the kitchen, and I was just reaching for the fridge when we heard "Just not Henry! Hi, Henry. Pleased to meet you, Henry. Not *Henri* but Henry!" And if that wasn't bad enough, then Ludwig let out a peal of laughter, like it was the funniest joke ever.

I couldn't help it. I giggled too.

Cabbage didn't think it was funny at all.

TEN

Uncle Eli was counting on me to do a good job with his bird. Plus, I needed to show Mom how responsible I was being about taking care of him. So on Sunday night I set my alarm for a half hour earlier than usual.

I got a good night's sleep—thanks to no middle-of-the-night bird drama—and even woke up a few minutes before my alarm. I turned it off and glanced over at my mold garden, which really was starting to stink. Nothing I could do about it right then, so I snuck out of my room with my clothes so as not to wake Chloe.

After I'd showered and dressed, I went into the dining room and flicked on the light.

"Good morning, Ludwig!" I said in my most friendly voice. He didn't say anything back but fluffed his feathers, and I could tell he was paying attention, eyeing me intently.

I chatted to him as I gave him fresh water, food and his tablespoon of vitamin powder. Instead of eating my breakfast in the kitchen, I set a place in the dining room and ate beside him as I talked and told him about my day ahead. I even gave him a Cheerio from my bowl (a dry one—Uncle Eli had said not to give him any dairy) through the cage bars and watched as he ate it. I thought it was kind of gross that he held it with his foot, which he used like a hand, holding the piece of cereal as he took little nibbles of it while standing on the other foot. But I figured it wasn't like he had a choice in how to eat it, since wings don't exactly have fingers. The more I watched, the more I realized how cool it was that he used his foot like a hand. He was such a dainty eater!

"Sorry that I have to be away for most of the day, Ludwig," I said in between mouthfuls of cereal. "But at least you have your toys to play with. Hopefully that will keep you busy so you won't be bored or lonely."

He had stopped eating his Cheerio and stood there with it held in his toes while he stared at me. Then, once I was done speaking, he returned to eating.

"You seem to be very interested in what I'm saying. I wish I could tell if you understand anything. Probably not," I said. "Anyway, maybe next week I can take you to school for show-and-tell. Marni brought Prince—her Labradoodle—so I know we're allowed to bring pets."

As I chewed another spoonful of Cheerios, I thought more about the idea of taking him to school. At first I got excited about showing him off to my class—no one had ever brought a bird for show-and-tell. But then I realized it might actually not be the best idea. "Now that I think about it, you'd probably get scared and growl at people and maybe even bite, so maybe I'll leave you at home, huh?"

Ludwig just looked at me, but I had a feeling he'd agree if he knew what I was saying.

After breakfast, once I was ready for school, I grabbed my backpack and stopped in front of his cage. "Have a great day, Ludwig! Don't miss me too much!" I said with a big smile as he stared silently back at me.

It wasn't until I was in the front hall, putting on my shoes, that I heard him say, "Thirty-four!" and then he laughed.

I had no idea what it meant. Probably nothing, but it made me smile anyway.

Since the tryouts for the Science Bowl were on Thursday, Cabbage and I had made plans to study together after school. After final period we rushed to the library, and while I grabbed books on random science subjects (geography, magnets, the human body, plants), Cabbage downloaded and printed out a bunch of practice Science Bowl questions. We would quiz each other during study breaks.

We were at one of the round tables, going through the books, when I felt a presence beside me. I looked up to see Brian Newman. He was taller than most other seventh graders and had curly brown hair that was always messy because he had a habit of raking his fingers through it. He was smart and nice *and* handsome. Which I guess was why Marni had decided she had to be his girlfriend.

"Hi, Arden, Henri," he said, a friendly smile on his face. Behind him stood Marni, a not-so-friendly scowl on hers. He might have been smart, nice and handsome, but he seemed to have weird (bad!) taste in girlfriends.

I looked from Marni to Brian. "Hi," I said. To him only.

"Are you studying for the Science Bowl?"

"A little. Mostly we're getting some books to take home," Cabbage said. "You're trying out, aren't you?"

Brian nodded, though he didn't look very confident. "You two study a lot, huh?"

"Yes," I said, pretending I didn't see Marni making faces behind Brian's back. Was she mean even to *him*? When she glanced over at me, I darted my eyes away, feeling my face heat up.

"Ugh, Brian, why would you want to do something as dorky as Science Bowl?" she barked, answering the question I hadn't bothered asking. Of course she was mean to him too!

He turned to look at her and frowned. "It's not dorky. Plus, if we win, we'll get to go to STEM camp."

"Dork camp, you mean." Marni tossed her hair. "But whatever. I'm not going to sit around with these geeks. Come on, let's get out of here."

"I'm not stopping you from leaving," Brian said, his voice low. He was obviously angry. He pursed his lips together for a long moment and then said, "In fact, I think you *should* go."

She put a hand on her hip and tilted her head. "You're kidding, right?"

"No, I'm not kidding," he said. "And if all you are going to do is insult me and other people who like the same things I do, I don't want to hang out with you anymore."

She clucked her tongue and rolled her eyes.

"I'm serious, Marni," Brian said. "Maybe *you* should try studying for once? And not being so mean to everyone? Why can't you be more like Arden?"

Marni gasped, and then her face froze in shock as what he'd said sunk in.

Because Brian had just said he wished Marni was more like me.

Then he turned away from her and toward us. "Mind if I study with you guys?"

Forgetting all the Marni drama (not easy to do when she was standing right there scowling, and Brian had just said what he had), I wasn't sure that letting him study with us was a good idea. I mean, if he studied a lot, he could beat one of us out for a spot on the team. Cabbage and I looked at each other, but then I suddenly had the thought that if he studied with us, we'd know what he was good at and whether he was a real threat. Cabbage must have read my mind, because he nodded and said, "Sure. That sounds great."

Marni suddenly unfroze. "Wait a minute," she said, her voice a lot squeakier than normal. "Did you just break up with me?"

Brian had been about to drop into the chair beside me but turned back to Marni, looking at her like he was surprised she was still there. "I can't see why that would be a problem since I'm *so dorky*. Goodbye, Marni."

I almost cheered but instead exchanged another wide-eyed look with Cabbage. Then Brian sat down with his back to her. He was clearly done with their relationship.

Marni had tears in her eyes as she huffed and stormed off, making me feel a little sorry for her. But only a little. Because popular, cute, smart Brian Newman had just asked her why she couldn't be more like me.

Later that night, after dinner, I returned to the dining room to do my homework and noticed a pile of grocery-store flyers stacked on the sideboard. Mom must have brought them home. I was glad she'd remembered to grab them, since I needed to tidy up Ludwig's cage and didn't have any more test papers to use.

I pulled out the tray at the bottom of the cage to get at the old papers, then realized I needed a garbage bag to put them in. I pushed the tray back in and went into the kitchen, which is when Ludwig started talking. "Thirty-four, thirty-four, THIRTY-FOUR!"

Silly bird! What the heck was *thirty-four*?

By the time I'd returned, he'd stopped talking and was now just staring, his silvery-white eyes intent on me. "What does that mean?" I asked, but he had no answer. I exhaled loudly and crouched down to pull the tray out. When I did, he climbed down the side of his cage to stand on the bars at the bottom. He twisted his neck to watch with one eye what I was doing.

"I'm just cleaning up the papers, Ludwig," I said in my calm voice. "Since you pooped on these ones." There were also lots of shredded wood bits (from the toys he'd been chewing up) and some discarded pellets—Uncle Eli hadn't been kidding when he said birds were messy! But he'd said there was a good reason for their being slobs: when they ate and scattered their mess around the rainforest, seeds got planted. He said birds were nature's gardeners, doing the important job of ensuring the constant regrowth of the plants, which I thought was pretty cool.

"Although I don't think we need pellet trees growing in our carpet," I muttered as I picked up as much of his food from the floor around his cage as I could and shoved it into the garbage bag.

"Ha ha!" Ludwig said suddenly, making me look up at him.

His laughter made me smile, especially because it sounded exactly like Uncle Eli's laugh. "Did you get that joke?" I asked, but he just looked at me.

Returning to my task, I pulled out the tray and noticed the poop on my old math test. I was a little sorry it was garbage now, since I'd done so well on it. Other than a single question I'd gotten wrong—the one that had a big red X beside it. I looked at the equation, working it out in my head as I gathered all the papers into a ball.

When I'd written the test, I'd come up with sixteen as the answer. But now, as I looked at it again, I knew that was wrong. I went through the equation again and this time got…wait. Thirty-four.

What? I looked up at the bird.

Thirty-four.

"Are you kidding me?" I said to the bird. No, it couldn't be. My brain was playing tricks on me. I looked at the equation again and worked it out a second time. This time I got... thirty-four. I took out my phone and texted Cabbage. **Do you still have the last math test? What was the answer for question seven?**

He must have been right by his phone. **Hold on,** he texted. He sent another message a minute later. **Thirty-four.**

No. Freaking. Way.

I looked up at the bird. "Do you know how to read? Do you know *math*?"

He just blinked at me.

"Ludwig!" I said. "This is *really* important!"

Blink, blink.

I stared at him for what felt like hours until Mom came into the room. "What are you doing, Arden? It's almost time for bed."

I didn't want to tell her about the math test, because if I was wrong, it would make me look ridiculous. If I was right, well, *that* was ridiculous. Birds couldn't do math. Could they? How on earth could *a bird* do a math test? But as Uncle Eli had always told me, I had to question everything—to look for answers no matter how ridiculous the questions. I had to figure it out somehow.

It was time to employ more of the scientific method, step one. Observation. Lots of observation.

Meanwhile my mother was waiting for an answer. "I'm just cleaning his cage," I said, busying myself doing that and not letting on that something really weird had just happened.

"Arden?" Mom asked. "What's wrong? Why are your hands shaking?"

"They aren't!" I said, shoving the balled-up math test into the garbage bag, keeping my hands moving. "I'm just doing his cage."

"Did he bite you?" she asked, leaning closer.

"No," I said. "I've just never done this before. It's fine! I'm fine! Everything is fine!"

Carefully avoiding her eyes, I could feel her watching me as I took my time opening up a grocery-store flyer and arranging the pages in the tray so they covered the whole thing.

Finally she left the room.

I looked up at the bird once I'd finished with the newspaper. "What is going on?" I whispered, not wanting Mom to overhear.

Blink, blink.

After another long moment, I sighed. Whatever was going on with the bird, he sure wasn't talking now.

I finished with the cage and got up, giving him one last look before I flicked off the dining-room light. "Good night, Ludwig," I said.

He didn't wish me a good night, but as I left the dining room, I distinctly heard him say, "One ninety-nine!" followed, of course, by birdy laughter.

I sighed in relief. There hadn't been a question on the test with an answer of one hundred and ninety-nine. Obviously thirty-four had been a coincidence. Right? Still, it was a weird coincidence. A *very* weird coincidence.

It was time to text my uncle.

I didn't want to bother Uncle Eli when he was on his way to the west coast of Africa (of course, I'd looked up where Guinea was), but I definitely needed to talk to him about Ludwig. Maybe it had only been a coincidence, but I couldn't stop thinking that it seemed an awful lot like the bird could not only read but also do math problems. I'd read that birds were smart and loved solving puzzles, but not one of the books had said anything about them being *that* smart!

And his solving a math equation (one *I* had gotten wrong!) definitely qualified as something weird and out of the ordinary.

On my way to my room to send him a text, I stopped at the entrance to the living room, where my mom was watching TV. "Have you heard from Uncle Eli?" I asked.

She shook her head. "Not yet. He said he's going to be traveling for several days to get to his base camp in Guinea. Why?"

"No biggie," I said with a shrug. "I was just going to let him know how Ludwig's doing. I'm sure he's very concerned."

She snorted. "He's probably more concerned about getting there in one piece, but you can text him, and I'm sure he'll respond when he can—remember he said he won't always be accessible. I can't imagine there's great cell service in the bush."

"I know," I said and turned to leave.

"Arden?"

I stopped and looked back at my mom.

"You're going to miss him, huh?"

Didn't she know that I already *did* miss him? My throat got tight as I nodded. Cabbage was my best friend, but Uncle Eli was my best uncle—he was the perfect combo of friend *and* family member. I cleared my throat and said, "Yes. But Ludwig laughs like him, so sometimes it feels like he's still here."

She smiled at that and then frowned. "Wait, you have your science thing this week, don't you?"

I took a deep breath, trying not to get nervous thinking about it. "Yeah. Cabbage and I have been studying a lot."

"I'm sure you'll do great," she said. "I'm really proud of you for how hard you're working at it. You and your uncle are a lot alike."

"Thanks," I said with a smile because it was a great compliment. "I guess I'd better get to bed."

Mom nodded, and I was about to leave when we heard "Thirty-four!" from the dining room.

We both laughed. "What a silly bird!" Mom said.

Silly bird or *genius* bird?

It took me forever to figure out what to say to Uncle Eli. Should I tell him the bird had solved a math equation? Did I really think he *had* solved an equation? It seemed impossible.

I questioned it over and over—could a bird count or do math? I didn't think so. That was the kind of stuff you saw in Disney movies right before the animal started singing.

So after a while I sent: **Hi! Hope your travel is ok. Ludwig update: no bites, all ok, Ludwig is so smart. Maybe super smart? txt back!**

I was disappointed that I didn't get a response right away. I wasn't too surprised, but I really wanted to talk to him. I just hoped it wouldn't take a long time for him to get back to me.

It did.

It wasn't until Wednesday morning that he finally sent a message. Even then, it wasn't a text directly to me but an email to my mom to say there was no cell service where he was. He would have to go into the village, where there was Wi-Fi, every so often to get supplies, so to get hold of him I should email instead of text. Mom said he'd asked how I was doing and she'd told him everything was fine and Ludwig was fine and the whole world was fine—which, of course, didn't help me at all.

ELEVEN

The Science Bowl tryouts were Thursday after school, which meant they were all I dreamed about the night before, questions and answers whirling through my head. And then at breakfast on Thursday morning, I'd had to beg Brandon to quiz me from science flash cards. It had cost me three nights of taking over his dish duty, but whatever. Worth it to be as prepared as I could be.

Cabbage and I tested each other all the way to school, and even in class I was constantly running through questions in my head. Thankfully, my teachers knew what was going on, so I didn't get in trouble when I zoned out and didn't participate like usual.

I was so focused that when Marni came up to me in the bathroom at the end of lunch period, while I was washing my hands, I hadn't even noticed she was in there.

Until she got right into my bubble, scowling as she said, "I need to talk to you."

Oh no. Was this about what Brian had said? A ball of dread formed in my gut as I stood there waiting. "I need to get on the Science Bowl team," she said.

I erupted in laughter because I'd thought she'd said she needed to get on the Science Bowl team. It was one of the funniest things I'd ever heard. But then I looked at her in the mirror and realized that's *exactly* what she'd said. She was dead serious.

"I'm dead serious," she said, like she'd read the words out of my brain. "I need to get on the team so I can get back with Brian."

So she really isn't kidding. Ugh.

"Well, good luck with that," I said snarkily (although it came out a little screechily). I had no idea what she'd been doing since Cabbage and I had watched Brian break up with her on Monday, but I doubted it was studying. The three of us, however—Cabbage, Brian and I—had been in the library every day, studying and quizzing each other.

"And anyway, why would you want to be on the team after you went on and on about how dorky Science Bowl is?"

"Because if I'm on the team, Brian will know I'm smart— because I am, you know!—and he'll want to be my boyfriend again," she said matter-of-factly. "And then when we win, we'll get to go to dork camp together."

Wait a minute. He'd asked her why she couldn't be more like me. *That's* what this was about. She wanted to act like me to get him back. Not that she'd ever admit it. Except that I was pretty sure he didn't like her at all anymore.

I turned off the tap and shook my hands over the sink to get the water off. "It's *STEM* camp, but whatever. You can try out like everyone else after school today." Not that she'd get on the team in a million years.

"Oh, I'm going to try out," she said, giving me her signature Meanie Marni glare in the mirror. "And you'd better not get in my way."

What? I turned toward her as my heart started racing. She was looming over me, and when I tried to step back, my butt hit the sink. I had nowhere to go. I was trapped.

She wasn't much bigger than me, but that didn't mean she couldn't push me down or hit me. And if she did, there was no one in the bathroom to help me or go for a teacher. "What does that mean? In your way of *what*?" She was the one who had me cornered in the bathroom.

She came closer, so close that her face was all blurry, before she said, "Just that I'd better make it onto the team one way or another."

Did she think I had any control over tryouts? As she continued to scowl at me, I noticed her breath smelled like onions. "Or what?"

"Or you'll find out," she said. "That's what. Remember what happened to Carolyn when she got in my way during volleyball?"

I gasped. Carolyn had fallen and sprained her ankle during volleyball tryouts, so she hadn't made the team. Marni had taken her place. It suddenly made so much sense. "You said bumping into her was an accident!"

Marni shrugged and then leaned forward again, making me squeeze my eyes shut as I braced for whatever it was she intended to do, which I was sure would be a lot worse than her blowing nasty oniony breath at me.

"Just stay out of my way," she whispered. "That's all I'm saying."

A second later I heard the squeak of the door, and when I opened my eyes, she was gone from the bathroom. But now she was totally in my head.

I was going to tell Cabbage what had happened with Marni, but what would I even say? He always said not to let her get to me and would just tell me again to ignore her. He didn't seem to get it.

Anyway, there was no way she'd make the team. She barely paid attention in class most of the time, let alone did any extra studying, and the tryouts were right after the final class that day.

"What is *she* doing here?" Brian said as he, Cabbage and I walked into the auditorium where the tryouts were being held.

I didn't even have to follow his gaze to know Marni was sitting in the front row.

"I guess she's trying out," I said, as though this was the first I knew of it too.

"Why?" Brian said.

I looked over at him. "Probably to impress you."

He snorted at that, and I almost felt sorry for Marni that her plan was going to totally backfire. Well, maybe I was looking forward a tiny bit to watching her mess up horribly.

Plus, she and Brian made zero sense together. He was so nice, and she was so the opposite.

We took seats in the auditorium and waited for Mr. Yan—our math teacher and the Science Bowl coach—to start the tryouts. He was already up on the stage, sitting at a table, looking down at a stack of papers.

A few more kids were still filing in behind us. I got more disheartened with each one that came in, wishing there wasn't so much competition.

"Wow, I didn't think there would be so many," Brian said, echoing my thoughts. "Lots of eighth graders too."

He looked as nervous as I felt. So did Cabbage, which just made me even more nervous.

"All right, everyone," Mr. Yan said as he stood up and waved in the last stragglers by the door. "It's time to get started, especially since we have so many of you trying out. We're going to call you up one by one, and you'll each get five questions. At the end we'll tally up the scores, and if we have any ties, we'll do another round until we have our team. Any questions?"

As a couple of kids put up their hands, I glanced over at Marni. She was staring at me, eyes narrowed. I looked away quickly, my heart pounding in my chest. I had to take a deep breath, but it didn't do any good to calm me down. What was her deal? Did she think I was the only thing standing in the way of her getting on the team? That was bonkers.

"I hope I'm first," Brian whispered.

"Are you kidding?" I asked. "Why on earth would you want to go first?"

His eyes widened. "To get it over with. I'm sort of freaking out already, and the longer I sit here, the more nervous I get."

It was a good point, though I preferred to go last. That way I could watch all the—

"Arden Sachs?" Mr. Yan called out and then looked around the audience until he found me. He gave me a smile when he did. "You're up first."

So much for going last. I groaned and got out of my chair as Cabbage and Brian both wished me good luck. I went up the five steps at the side of the stage and took my seat at the table while the million kids in the auditorium watched. I wished I'd gone to the bathroom, because I suddenly felt like I *really* had to go. Stupid nervous bladder.

"Ready?" Mr. Yan asked as he shuffled his papers.

No. But I would never be *more* ready, so I nodded. Then something in the audience caught my eye. I glanced down to see Marni and Shannon sitting together, staring up at me. Marni narrowed her eyes at me again and shook her head menacingly. She didn't need to say even one word for me to understand that she was telling me I'd better not beat her out for a spot on the team. I glanced over at Cabbage, who was smiling at me encouragingly. One of the few times he couldn't read my mind to know I was freaking out—he was totally clueless.

"Arden?" Mr. Yan said, pulling my attention back to him.

"Sorry," I said. "I'm ready."

"All right, first question. At what temperature does water boil?"

That was an easy one! Relieved, I smiled and said, "One hundred degrees Celsius and two hundred and twelve degrees Fahrenheit."

"Correct."

I smiled, happy that I'd started out so well. But then I heard someone clear their throat *very* loudly. That someone was Marni. And she was glaring at me as if she could shoot lasers out of her eyes. She did that little headshake again. What would she do if I beat her out? I thought back to when Uncle Eli had made me promise to tell on her if she hurt me physically. But would she really hurt me if I got on the team and she didn't? That would get her in a lot of trouble...but by then it might be too late—the damage would be done. I liked all my bones and flesh intact, thank you very much.

And, of course, there were more ways she could hurt me. She already made me miserable with her nasty words and threats. Calling me names and looming over me all the time. If I beat her out for a spot on the team, she'd never leave me alone.

"Arden?" Mr. Yan said. "Do you need me to repeat the question?"

Gah! "Yes, please," I said, turning back toward him, trying to ignore the fact that Marni was watching me. Glaring at me. Sending her hate molecules at me. Not that she knew what a molecule was, but even so I could feel them pelting me as I sat there.

"All right, pay attention. I will only repeat myself once."

I nodded, forcing myself to focus.

"What are the icicle-shaped deposits of limestone that hang from the roof of a cave called?"

Marni cleared her throat again, this time louder, and then she added a cough that sounded a lot like "volleyball." She was reminding me what had happened to Carolyn. And what could happen to me.

What do I do? Cabbage would tell me to ignore her, and Uncle Eli would tell me to tattle on her. But neither of them had been in the bathroom when she threatened me, and neither of them were inside my head right now.

I swallowed, took a deep breath and said, "Stalagmites."

Mr. Yan winced and pursed his lips. "I'm sorry, that's incorrect. It's *stalactites*."

I could feel Cabbage's eyes on me, and I knew he wondered what was going on, because we'd studied caves on the weekend and we'd even done a unit on them in class. He knew I knew the right answer. Maybe he thought I'd just made a nervous error. It was easy enough to do—the words were really similar. That's what I'd tell him had happened.

"Okay, moving on. Where would you find the smallest bones in the human body?"

"Toes?" I said, making it seem like I wasn't sure. But I was very sure. I was completely and totally 100 percent sure that toes was the wrong answer.

"I'm sorry, that's incorrect. The smallest bones in the human body are in the ear."

I blew out a loud breath, feeling all eyes on me, judging me, thinking I was stupid. Just two more questions, I told myself, and then you can run out of here and pretend it never happened, that Science Bowl doesn't even exist, that you won't care about not making the team or going to STEM camp.

"All right. What is the cube root of eight?"

A math question? Cabbage would know for sure that I knew this one. I coughed as I said, "Four," because maybe then he wouldn't hear.

"Could you repeat your answer, please?" the teacher asked.

"Four?" I repeated in a small voice.

"I'm sorry, but the correct answer is two," Mr. Yan said.

I cringed, like I had no idea four was wrong.

"And last question," Mr. Yan said, giving me a pitying look that made me pray for a sudden sinkhole right there in the middle of the auditorium. "A mass of ice, formed by the compaction and recrystallization of snow, that is constantly moving either downhill or outward under the force of gravity is called what?"

I swallowed again as I realized I would have totally aced every single one of these questions if it hadn't been for Marni. I was about to say *iceberg*, to completely ruin my chances of getting on the team, but I didn't want everyone—especially Cabbage and Brian—to think I didn't know *anything*.

"Glacier," I said, watching as Mr. Yan exhaled in relief.

"Correct," he said. "Two out of five. Thanks, Arden. Why don't you have a seat while we continue with the tryouts?" He looked down at his paper and then up toward the crowd. "Andy Fernandez, you're up next."

I got up and walked slowly down the steps to the audience. So many eyes were on me. Marni's and Shannon's but also Cabbage's as he glared at me, wondering what had just happened.

The tears were coming. I was heartbroken and embarrassed and other things that I couldn't even name. How could I explain what I'd just done? I couldn't. So instead of joining Cabbage and Brian in their seats, I just kept going to the doors at the back. Once I was through those, I ran down the hall and out of the school.

I didn't stop until I got to my condo building and had to dig out my key for the glass doors to the lobby.

Once I was off the elevator and in my condo, all I wanted to do was get to my room and bawl in peace, but I could hear Chloe in there listening to music. I was so not in the mood to have to explain to her what had happened or listen to her complain about my mold garden.

I went into the bathroom to clean myself up and take some time to calm down, but then Brandon banged on the door.

"Can't I have five minutes to myself?" I growled as I came out.

"What's up your butt?" Brandon said, but he didn't wait for my answer before pushing past me and slamming the door practically in my face. Jerk.

I went into the dining room, where Ludwig was standing on his branch like he'd been when I left for school. He hadn't eaten the treats in his puzzle toy, and I wondered if it was too hard for him (it had taken me forever to get the almonds and bits of dehydrated mango *into* it). He did his little feather-fluffing shake and then yawned, the little ritual I had come to think of as his way of saying hello.

"Hi, Ludwig," I said, sounding very sad even to my own ears.

I wondered if he could tell or if he even knew what it meant to be sad. I hoped he'd never been sad, but at the same time I also wished he could understand how I was feeling. He tilted his head to look at me with his right eye, straight on, like he was trying to figure me out. Like I was his puzzle toy or something.

"I had a pretty awful day," I said.

The bird came down to his rope perch, which brought him right to the front of his cage.

"I completely messed up the Science Bowl tryouts," I said as he sat there quietly watching me like he was really paying attention to what I was saying. "And the worst part is, I did it on purpose. I let Meanie Marni intimidate me, and I got the answers wrong on purpose. Now I won't be on the team or go to STEM camp. And she's going to be..." Well, I didn't think she would actually get on the team. There would have to be a miracle for that to happen.

But whether she was on the team or not, I wouldn't be, and that was what really mattered. "Anyway," I said out loud, "I'm just sad about it, is all."

Ludwig turned around and climbed up the bars until he was back on his branch beside the puzzle toy. It made me even sadder that he seemed not to care and was suddenly more interested in his toy than me. Though I had to admit, I *was* sort of feeling sorry for myself, which made me not exactly fun to be around.

But then he went to the toy and used his beak to line up all its parts until an almond dropped to the tray at the bottom, which took *way* less time than it had taken me to get it in there. Then, with the almond in his mouth, he climbed back down to the rope perch and stuck his beak between the bars, holding the nut out toward me.

"Is that for me?" I asked, tears flooding my eyes. "Really?"

Maybe my eyes were all blurry and I just wanted to see it, but I could have sworn he nodded. I took the almond from him and nibbled at it, not because I wanted it but because he'd obviously done what he thought would cheer me up. Uncle Eli had said birds were really sensitive and could read energy. Ludwig might not have understood *why* I was upset, but he sure seemed to know that I was.

As I took almost microscopic bites of the almond and observed him as he watched me, I was definitely back to thinking he was a genius. A really nice genius.

TWELVE

I'd run away from the school, but I couldn't run away from my best friend. Not as long as he had my phone number.

From the second I'd raced out of the auditorium after the disastrous Science Bowl tryouts, my phone had been pinging constantly with text messages from him. I'd ignored them and turned off the sound. I'd have to deal with him eventually, but not yet.

Because how could I explain what had happened? Marni didn't bother Cabbage as much as she bothered me, and I was sure she hadn't cornered *him*, telling him he'd better not beat her out of a spot on the team. He would have laughed in her face if she'd tried.

He wouldn't understand how much she got to me.

I was mad at her for being so mean. I was mad at myself for letting her get to me. More than anything, though, I was ashamed.

When there was a knock on the front door just as we were finishing dinner, I was sure it was him. I "accidentally" spilled the rest of my juice down my top and asked Mom to tell him I had to go change and would talk to him the next morning. Instead of changing, though, I hid around the corner to hear the conversation.

"Oh," I heard him say after she'd explained. "She left the tryouts in a hurry today. I just wanted to make sure everything was okay."

"Tryouts?" Mom asked as I cringed.

"For the Science Bowl," Cabbage said.

"Oh, that's right!" Mom said. "She didn't mention it." I could hear the worry in her voice and knew she and I would be having a talk about it. "Although she did seem quieter than normal at dinner. I'm guessing it didn't go well."

"No." My best friend sighed. "She didn't do very well at all. Maybe she's coming down with something and that put her off her game?"

Mom paused, and I got ready to run to my bedroom, worried she was going to beckon me to the front hall to explain myself. Instead she said to Cabbage, "Maybe. Anyway, thanks for checking in, Henri. Say hi to your parents for me, okay?"

I hurried into my room so I wouldn't get caught eavesdropping in the hall. I quickly changed into my pajamas and jumped into bed, pulling the covers up to my chin. I realized I'd left my phone in my jeans, so I got that out and put it face-down on my nightstand—I still hadn't turned it on and could only imagine the messages I had waiting for me. I'd deal with those after I'd dealt with my mother.

Who then appeared in the doorway.

"Hey, Arden," she said. "Want to tell me why you're avoiding Henri?"

I couldn't completely lie and tell her I was sick, but I didn't exactly want to tell her everything that had happened either. "I blew the tryouts," I said, which was the truth.

"Aw, honey." She came into the room and sat beside me on my bed. "You were working so hard. I'm sorry it didn't go well."

As I fought back tears, I just nodded, not looking at her.

"Are you upset because Henri got on the team and you didn't?"

I did look at her then, because her question made me realize I had no idea who had made it onto the team. I assumed Cabbage had, but I'd been so wrapped up in my own stuff that I hadn't thought to find out. That made me feel bad—I really did want him to ace the tryouts and get on the team.

"No," I said and then had to clear my throat. "It's not like that. I'm just sad that I blew it." *On purpose*, I didn't add. *And Marni is such an awful human being and she hates me for no reason.* I didn't add that either.

Mom squeezed my hand, and I almost started really crying. "I'm so sorry," she said. "What can I do?"

Not talk about it? Pretend none of this happened? Send me to Guinea to be with Uncle Eli? I kept my suggestions to myself. She didn't even know about Marni, since the only grown-up I'd ever told was Uncle Eli.

I hadn't even planned to tell him, but one day when we were at the Science Museum, checking out all the cool displays, he'd told me he was bullied when he was my age. All because he loved science. When I'd asked him about Mom—his twin—he'd laughed and shaken his head, telling me she had been one of the popular girls at school.

So no, she wouldn't understand.

I just shrugged.

Mom was quiet for a few minutes, and I could tell she was trying to think of some way to cheer me up. I was about to tell her nothing would work when she said, "Why don't we go to the mall this weekend? I know I've been working a lot lately, so let's go do something together. I could use a few new tops, and we can get lunch, maybe get our nails done. We can even go to the pet store." She knew if anything could cheer me up, that was it.

I thought about Ludwig and how he'd given me his almond. "Maybe we can get Ludwig something special?"

She leaned over and kissed my forehead. "That sounds like a good idea. Maybe it will make him feel better about your uncle being away." Then she added, "Not that you aren't doing a great job with him."

"I know," I said, feeling more confident about Ludwig than I ever would have expected. Like maybe looking after him wasn't the worst thing after all.

"I must say, I'm relieved I haven't had to patch up any flesh wounds," Mom said. "And we haven't had any evac alarms since that first night."

This made me smile. "No," I said. "He's not as bad as I first thought he'd be."

"Good," she said and then gave me another forehead kiss

before she pushed up off my bed. "And I know your uncle is proud of you for taking him even though he wasn't the pet you were hoping for." She looked at me sideways and added, "But don't get any ideas—he's going back once Uncle Eli returns."

"I know, Mom," I said.

She stopped in the doorway, her hand on the frame as she glanced over at my clock. "It's pretty early to go to bed."

"May as well." Since tryouts were over and I wasn't on the team, I didn't have studying to do. For once I didn't feel like studying just for fun.

"Aw, Arden, don't pout. Come watch *The Bachelor* with me."

I scrunched up my face at my mother's love of awful reality TV. "Really? *The Bachelor*?" You didn't even learn anything watching it. Not anything good anyway.

"Fine!" she exclaimed with a big roll of her eyes. "It's how I relax and turn my brain off after a long day, but obviously that's too lowbrow for you, my brainy daughter, so I'll let you put on the Discovery Channel."

"Deal," I said, grinning as I got out of bed and slid my feet into my slippers.

Even though I was dragged out after the drama of the day before, the next morning started with my new routine of getting up before everyone else. As I chatted to him, I dumped out Ludwig's leftover pellets, cleaned his dishes and then refilled them, one with water and the other with his food and vitamin mixture. Once he was all set for the day, I sat myself down at the dining-room table to eat *my* breakfast. By then Mom was in the shower, but Chloe and Brandon were still in bed, both of them late sleepers—or as late as they could make it without missing school.

While I ate, I watched as Ludwig took a pellet in his beak and walked it over to his water dish. He dropped it in and then fished it out and ate it.

It seemed weird until I looked down at my bowl of Cheerios and milk. "Huh. I guess I don't like dry cereal either."

He went back to his food dish, picked up a single red, crescent-shaped pellet, took it back to the water dish and dunked.

"At least I know now how the pellets get in your water."

He looked at me (knowingly?) and ate his pellet, crunching it in his beak. I remembered how I'd read that birds think of eating as a flock activity.

"Do you like us having breakfast together, Ludwig?" I asked.

He didn't answer but picked a round orange pellet out of his dish and dropped it into his water.

"Slam dunk!" I said, because the pellet almost looked like a tiny basketball. And he was dunking it, after all.

He did a funny dance move, shaking his tail feathers. It almost looked like a victory dance.

That made me giggle. And then *he* laughed. Which made me giggle even more.

It went on for a long time like that, until my sides hurt.

But it was a good way to start the day.

When it came time to meet Cabbage for school, I was nervous. I'd read all the messages he'd sent me—some were from the tryouts:

RDen?
What happened? You KNEW those answers!
Where did you go?
RDen? What's going on?
RU OK?

And then there were several that came in later and into the evening, after he'd talked to my mom. Mostly they were him telling me he hoped I was feeling better and to let him know if I wasn't going to school and he'd get my homework for me. He was such a good friend, which made it even more awkward.

I'd even considered faking sick to stay home so I wouldn't have to see him, Brian, Mr. Yan and especially Marni. Mom would never have bought it, though.

I peeked out the peephole when I heard a door in the hallway close and took a deep breath when I saw it was him. I left my condo, locking it behind me.

"Hey, Arden?" Cabbage said with a frown as he came up to me quickly, hitching his backpack up on his shoulders. "Everything okay? I've been really worried about you."

"Oh, um, I…" I sighed, not having any idea what to say.

"What happened yesterday?" he asked. We got to the elevator, and he pushed the button. "Were you sick? Did you have a fever or something?"

That might have explained my wrong answers. "No," I said, wishing I could lie to my best friend. It would be so much easier than telling him the embarrassing truth.

He tilted his head, but just then the elevator came. We got on and as he pressed the G button, I looked at the numbers, watching them light up in order, hoping maybe he'd change the subject. Or forget we'd been having a conversation at all.

He didn't.

"Arden?" he said when we were nearly halfway down to the ground floor. "What made you mess up those answers?"

I looked over at him and opened my mouth, but then the elevator lurched to a stop at the sixth floor. The doors opened, giving me a minute to stall. A man in a suit, carrying a briefcase, stepped on and gave us a polite smile and a muttered "Good morning."

"Hi," Cabbage said as I nodded at the man. Cabbage then turned back to me, his eyebrows up high on his head.

"Fine," I said on a loud exhale. "Marni."

He did a double take, like he hadn't heard me. "What?"

I glanced at the back of the man standing in front of me and then shook my head at my friend. "Later."

Cabbage didn't look happy about that, but he didn't have long to wait. *Later* happened when we got to the lobby and the doors opened. The man took a right toward the parking garage, and that left the two of us alone again.

"What do you mean, *Marni*?" Cabbage said.

I swallowed and pushed open the first glass door and then the second glass door—the one to the outside—before I started walking really fast.

"Arden? Hold on," he said, coming up beside me. He grabbed my arm when I didn't slow down. "What's going on?"

I stopped then and turned to face my best friend. "She told me she wanted to get on the team and I had better not stand in her way."

"What does that mean?" His eyes went wide. "Wait. She threatened you?"

I nodded, fighting back the tears. I didn't want him to see me cry. I don't know why—I just didn't.

"Why didn't you tell me?" he asked, looking hurt. "Or Mr. Yan?"

I dropped my eyes, looking down at the pavement. "I don't know," I muttered. It was a lie, because of course I knew why I hadn't told him. He wouldn't understand. He'd think I was stupid or weak for not standing up to her.

"Arden," he said, squeezing my arm. Not hard, but to get my attention. "Why didn't you tell me? Why didn't you tell the teacher?"

I shrugged and pulled my arm from his grasp. "I don't know, Cabbage, okay?"

"Wait a minute," he said, his voice getting louder all of a sudden. "You didn't get the questions wrong because you were nervous and made mistakes. You got them wrong *on purpose*. You let her bully you into throwing your tryout."

Obviously! But I couldn't say it out loud. I just stared at him. Then the worst thing happened. He got mad. Really mad. "You ruined the team. You could have beat her, Arden! How could you let her do that?"

Wait, what?

His eyes were wide, and he got right in my face. "She's on the team, Arden. Because *you* messed up. Somehow she made it onto the team!"

For a smart girl, I was struggling to understand what he was telling me. "What? How is that possible? With all those kids there? All the eighth graders even?"

He snorted and shook his head as he looked down the street. "There were so many kids trying out that Mr. Yan made two teams—one for seventh graders and one for eights. Somehow she got four out of her five questions right."

"How? She didn't study. She doesn't know *any* of that stuff!"

He shrugged. "Well, she did yesterday. Although it wouldn't have mattered that she did if you hadn't blown it. You knew all five of yours, didn't you?"

It didn't matter that he was right. It didn't matter because it was too late. She was now on the team, which was exactly what she'd wanted. And the worst part was, I'd made it happen because I'd let her scare me into ruining my tryouts. And now my best friend was mad at me, which seemed like the most unfair thing of all.

"We're never going to win now. We'll never get to STEM camp!"

That's when it *really* hit me. I hadn't just ruined my tryout. I had ruined my chance of ever going to STEM camp. Probably Cabbage's too, since with Marni on the team, there was no way they'd ever win. But it wasn't my fault!

"Why are you mad at *me*?" I said, my face crumpling when I couldn't hold the tears back anymore. "*She's* the mean one! *She's* the one who's a bully! Why aren't you mad at *her*?"

He crossed his arms. "Because you could have stopped her."

"That is not fair!" Tears were rolling down my cheeks. "*You* weren't the one she cornered in the bathroom! You don't know what it was like when I was on the stage and she was making horrible, mean faces at me!" I shouted, not even caring that anyone on the street could hear me yelling and crying. "If you're mad at me because I didn't want to get hurt, then you're just as mean as she is!"

I didn't wait for an answer—not that he had one, as he was staring at me like I'd just sprouted three heads—and ran off toward the school.

THIRTEEN

By lunchtime it was obvious that Cabbage and I were no longer friends.

Since I'd bolted from him, he'd been doing his best to avoid me, which was fine. I mean, if he hadn't, I would have been doing *my* best to avoid *him*. Still, I might have stolen a few glances at him when he wasn't looking, noticing that he seemed to be besties with Brian now, which made me mad.

Speaking of Brian, he was doing *his* best to avoid Marni.

And Marni? After the morning announcements, when they'd told the whole school who was on the seventh-grade Science Bowl team—Brian, Cabbage, Charlotte Hughes and her—she'd been walking around like she owned the place, going on and on about how she'd made it. How this meant, obviously, that she was the smartest girl in seventh grade, if not the entire school.

Right. Even though she'd dumped on the Science Bowl just days earlier, had failed the last science test and nearly failed the last math quiz as well. *And* hadn't even gotten all five of her Science Bowl questions right, even though *I'd* known all five of mine.

Not that I could prove it, but…

Something wasn't right. Maybe it was time to go back to the scientific method. I'd already observed that she shouldn't have been able to get on the team. And I already had a question. How had she gotten those four answers right?

It was time for step three—form a hypothesis. And the one I came up with? She must have cheated.

It was the only way she could have done so well—I was sure of it. I just had no idea how I was going to prove it.

I'd never been so relieved to get to the final bell on a Friday in my life. School was complete and utter agony.

I'd held a tiny glimmer of hope that Cabbage would realize he'd been a jerk and would apologize on the walk home. Of course, I would forgive him, and we'd go back to being best friends again. But the second the final bell rang, he jumped out of his seat and ran out the door like his chair was on fire.

So much for the working-things-out plan.

As I sighed and made my way to my locker (just in time to see Cabbage practically sprinting down the hall and out the door of the school), Charlotte Hughes came up beside me. If she'd noticed Cabbage running away from me like I had a deadly virus, she didn't say anything, which was nice because

I didn't want to explain. Instead she gave me a sympathy face and said, "Sorry you didn't make it on the team."

"Thanks. And congrats that you did," I mumbled, not really wanting to talk about it. Maybe she'll go away if I don't say anything, I thought as I turned the dial on my lock very slowly.

No such luck. "I can't believe Marni made it on," she said in a whisper, looking over her shoulder. Obviously she didn't want to be overheard by any of the other kids. Marni wasn't around, but Shannon's locker was just two down from mine and she was there, putting books into her backpack.

"Me neither," I said and then had a thought. I abandoned my lock and looked up at her. "Did she…did she talk to you before tryouts?"

Charlotte frowned. "No. Why? What did she do?"

"Nothing," I lied. I wished I wasn't the only one Marni had targeted, but I had a feeling I was. Did she think Brian liked me? Was that the *real* reason she didn't want me on the team? I returned to my lock, thinking about the even bigger mystery. How had Marni done so well on tryouts? *Had* she cheated?

"Anyway," Charlotte said with a sigh, "she's the worst. I really wish it was you on the team with us. Brian and Henri are great, but *she's* going to be a nightmare to study and practice with, if you know what I mean."

I *did* know what she meant. "She beat out Andy too, huh?"

"Yeah," she said with another big sigh. "He's our alternate. I just can't believe she made it at all. Did she study with you guys?"

"No," I said, keeping my voice low. "She was talking about how dorky it was just a few days ago. She only wanted to be on the team so Brian would think she's smart."

Charlotte snorted and then looked over her shoulder again before she leaned in close and said, "Like that's going to work—I think he's more upset than anyone that she made it on the team."

He couldn't be more upset than I was. Not possible.

Although…now I wondered if *he* was mad at me too.

What a disaster.

That night I must have composed about thirty texts to Cabbage and erased every single one of them. I felt bad that we'd had a huge fight, but I was still mad at him for being so mean and unfair. Those two things were jumbled up in my head, leaving me with no idea what to say to him. Should I say sorry? Or did he owe *me* an apology? What if I said I was sorry first and then he *didn't* apologize?

It was easier just to say nothing. And it wasn't like he'd texted. Plus, a tiny part of me thought maybe he would be studying with Brian, and I didn't want to hear about it.

This meant that for the first time since I couldn't remember when, Cabbage and I had spent a whole day not talking.

At least I had a bird to rant to.

"So you see, Ludwig," I said to him after breakfast on Saturday morning. It was early—Mom was out for a run, and Chloe and Brandon were still in bed. I was sitting at the dining-room table, coloring the image of famous mathematician Ada Lovelace in my *Historical Heroines* coloring book that Uncle Eli had given me the previous Hanukkah. "It's all very complicated. I just hope we can work things out and go back to being best friends, though I'm not sure how."

I was really worried things would never be the same between Cabbage and me. That made me so sad, I could almost cry just thinking about it.

The bird made a sound, and I looked up at him. "Did you just snort at me?"

He turned his head and looked at me with one eye.

I went back to my coloring. "Whatever. I don't think you know what I'm saying."

He sighed. Or made a sighing sound—it was hard to tell if he was imitating the sound or doing it himself.

As I picked up a different marker, I wondered if birds sighed in the wild. I didn't know what kind of sounds birds made in their natural habitats, but I was pretty sure it wasn't microwave hums, fire alarms and human laughter.

That thought made me smile. I reached for my glass of milk, but it was empty. I got up for a refill, and as soon as I was in the kitchen, Ludwig spoke.

"Cabbage! Two for ninety-nine cents. This week only. Get yours while supplies last!"

I froze with my hand on the fridge-door handle. Was he saying stuff about cabbage because I'd been talking about my friend? Or…wait. He sounded like an advertisement.

Uncle Eli spent so much time at the college that it made sense he would read to the bird. But would he read him shopping flyers? No, he'd have chosen textbooks or maybe even poetry books. Definitely not shopping flyers.

Maybe Uncle Eli put on the radio or TV when Ludwig was alone. That would make sense. Anyway, it was a pretty funny thing for Ludwig to repeat.

Shaking my head, I pulled the fridge door open.

"Cabbage! Tomatoes! Grapes! Ker-chunk. Beep-beep-beep. Hmmmmmm, hmmmmmm. Beeeeeeep. Mmmmm, coffee!"

I returned to the dining room, and of course Ludwig clammed up as soon as he saw me. It was so frustrating that he wouldn't talk while I was in the room.

I happened to glance down at the papers in his cage. Just grocery flyers—but wait. Whoa! Heads of cabbage *were* on sale, two for ninety-nine cents.

What?! I blinked at the flyer and then looked up at the bird. No. It just wasn't possible. But how else could I explain it?

Between the flyer now and the math test before, I could only think that somehow, *somehow*, he was reading. Impossible!

Or was it?

I *so* needed to get hold of my uncle! I'd tried to text him again, but I'd still had no response. Now I had even more reason to talk to him. Ludwig's behavior definitely qualified as weird.

As I looked at Ludwig and he gave me the side-eye, I wondered if he understood that Cabbage was my friend. Or did he think I was ranting about how I'd messed things up with a cruciferous vegetable? While I didn't love actual vegetables, I didn't often argue with them. That thought made me laugh a little.

Which made Ludwig chuckle.

"You are *so* silly, Ludwig."

He did a little dance, proving my point.

Just then there was a knock at the door. I put down my milk and went to the front hall, looking out the peephole.

It was Cabbage.

What was he doing here? Was he here to yell at me? Was he still mad? Was *I* still mad at *him*? I didn't take time to even think about it. I took a big, deep breath and opened the door.

"Hi, Arden," he said in a sad voice. His hands were in the pockets of his jeans, and his shoulders were hunched. He didn't look mad, but he wasn't happy either. Well, that made two of us.

"Hi," I said back.

"Can I come in?"

I nodded and stood back, opening the door wider so he could get past me. "I'm in the dining room with Ludwig."

"So…Arden…we need to talk," he said, shuffling inside.

"Oh, okay," I said. *As long as you're not going to yell at me.* But looking at his face, I didn't think he was. I walked ahead of him to the dining room and sat in front of my coloring book.

"Hi, Ludwig," he said to the bird and then sat down in the chair opposite me.

Ludwig turned to stare at Cabbage with one eye but didn't say anything, which was a relief—I was worried he was going to call Cabbage Henry like he had before. But maybe he could tell that now was not the time for birdy jokes.

"So," Cabbage said. He didn't quite meet my eyes. "Uh… about yesterday."

I opened my mouth, then realized I had no idea what to say. I stayed quiet and waited. He'd come over because he had something he wanted to tell me, so he could go first.

"So, I…uh…I told my mom what happened. With Marni and the tryouts and everything."

WHAT? I was about to get really mad, but he must have seen that in my face, because he held up a hand and said, "Hold on, Arden. Don't freak out. Let me finish."

I clamped my mouth closed and nodded.

He went on. "I guess when you told me about Marni and what she did to you in the bathroom, it didn't really sink in at the time what that meant for you. I wasn't going to say anything to my mom, I promise, but when I got home, she knew something was wrong. She dragged out of me what happened."

Cabbage wasn't normally one to blab, so I believed him. But still, why did he have to tell his mom? Ugh.

"But it's actually a good thing that I told her," he added quickly, "because we had a long talk about it." He glanced at me and then looked down at the table before he continued. "She made me realize that what Marni did was really scary for you and I was not a good friend the way I reacted. I wasn't seeing it from your side, and you were right that I was unfair." He reached for one of my markers—my favorite purple one—and absently spun it around with his fingers.

I thought about what I was supposed to say to him. Nothing popped into my head, but he wasn't done talking anyway.

"She never should have threatened you—I mean, obviously I *knew* that, but now I understand why you felt like you had to fail the tryouts. You didn't feel like you had a choice."

My throat was so tight, I couldn't possibly speak, but I nodded.

"I'm so sorry, Arden," he said, his eyes all glassy when he finally looked up at me. "I…I honestly didn't understand how you were feeling. I never meant to hurt you or be a jerk about it or make it seem like your feelings were wrong. But I did, and I'm really sorry."

I took a gulp of my milk, which almost didn't make it past the giant lump in my throat before I could speak. "I know you didn't mean to hurt me. It's okay," I squeaked. Then added, "I forgive you."

"Thank you," he said with a nod, looking relieved. "But now we have to make this right."

I frowned. "How?" I asked. "It's too late. She's already on the team!"

He took a big breath and straightened his shoulders. "We have to tell Mr. Yan what she did."

What? "No way. I'm not tattling on her. That'll make it a million times worse." I'd thought he understood now. But if he did, he'd know that telling on her was the worst thing I could do.

"I thought about that," he said, determined. "But Arden, I think you need to be brave and do it. Stand up to her this time with a teacher—and me—at your back, and she'll learn you

104

won't take her junk anymore, that you're not scared of her. And maybe it'll stop her from doing it to other kids too."

"But I *am* scared of her, Cabbage," I said, my voice small. "You don't know what it was like when she came at me in the bathroom."

"I know," he said seriously. "But if you tell the school, they'll make sure she stops bullying you. You don't have to do this on your own, Arden. She cornered you in the bathroom by yourself because she knew she could intimidate you that way."

He was right, but…

"You're my best friend—I *always* have your back and should have known something was wrong."

It was a little overwhelming, what he was saying, but the most important thing was that he'd said I was his best friend.

I sighed. "I don't know why I'm so afraid of her," I said. "I wish I could be like you and not be."

He squared his shoulders. "You won't be afraid of her after we talk to Mr. Yan."

I wasn't so sure. "You don't think she'll get back at me if she gets in trouble?" Because if we told on her, she was *definitely* going to get in trouble.

"I don't think so," he said. "They're probably going to call her parents. But we should go to tell Mr. Yan before class, first thing on Monday."

"What's happening on Monday?" my mother asked as she came into the dining room. She was still in her running clothes, her face flushed and her hair a sweaty mess.

Cabbage looked at me and lifted his eyebrows. It was up to me to tell her.

Mom crossed her arms and leaned against the doorframe, waiting.

I figured I'd have to tell her sooner or later and might as well get it over with, even though my heart was racing and it was the absolute last thing I wanted to do.

I sighed and pointed at the chair at the end of the table. "Sit down, Mom. I need to tell you what really happened with the Science Bowl."

FOURTEEN

Mom totally freaked out. But not at me.

She was upset that I hadn't told her anything about Marni, of course, but mostly she was upset at what Marni had done, going all mama bear about it.

In the end she decided she was taking me to school on Monday to talk to the principal (because apparently we needed to talk to *her* about Marni, not just to Mr. Yan). So after I explained everything, she got up and called her boss, Dr. Stinson, telling her she had to take Monday morning off to deal with an "important personal issue."

I grimaced at Cabbage, who was flipping through my coloring book. "I hope she knows what she's doing," I said. "Talking to the principal is a big deal."

He nodded. "Your mom's got your back too."

Of course she did, and maybe I should have talked to her sooner. But still.

"You don't have to take me, Mom," I said when she'd ended

the call. "I can talk to the principal myself." Or not. I still wasn't sold on the idea. Because while Cabbage seemed pretty sure that telling a teacher would solve my Marni problem, my own hypothesis was that it wouldn't. Keeping things as they were seemed like the easier road—after all, Marni was already on the team. Telling on her and getting her in trouble would just make her hate me more.

"This is important, Arden," Mom said in her and-that's-final voice.

"I'm sorry you'll miss work," I said, feeling bad. She did work a lot, but I knew it was because she had to.

"Some things are more important than work. And anyway, with all the overtime I put in, they can find someone to fill in for a couple of hours." She sighed and pursed her lips before she said, "And if I wasn't so wrapped up in my job, I would have seen that something was wrong with you. Come here." She put her arms around me and pulled me in for a tight hug. It made me feel better about having told her and her missing work. But not about having to talk to the principal.

When I pulled away, she turned to Cabbage. "Thank you for being such a good friend to Arden. You're a nice kid, Henri."

"Mom," I said. "Awkward."

Cabbage's cheeks were a little pink as he nodded at my mom.

Mom turned back to me. "What time are we going to the mall?"

I shrugged. "Whenever."

"All right," she said. "I need a shower and at least another coffee, so how about eleven, and then we can grab some lunch?"

I sat back down at the table across from Cabbage. "Okay. That gives me time to finish my picture."

After Mom left, I plucked my coloring book from Cabbage's hands and carefully tore out my half-finished page before handing it back to him so he could choose a picture to do.

He settled on the page about Dorothea Bate, the paleontologist, and reached for a brown marker. "So what are you going to do for your show-and-tell speech this week?"

I sighed. My turn to do a speech was on Tuesday. Cabbage's was on Thursday, and he already had his all planned out. He was bringing in the model of a space shuttle that he'd made over the summer.

I'd never been one to leave projects to the last minute, but we'd been studying so much for the Science Bowl that I really hadn't thought of anything cool and meaningful to bring in. At least, nothing that Marni wouldn't sniff at. I couldn't help but think about her bringing in her adorable dog. How could I compete with that?

I shrugged. "I don't know. I guess I'd better come up with something."

"What about a picture of Ludwig and some of his pet supplies? You could talk about your uncle's research and how you're taking care of him," Cabbage suggested.

"A picture?" I made a face. "Please." Because Marni had brought her *actual* dog. Her adorable and friendly dog. Who everyone had loved. I thought again about how great it would be to bring Ludwig, but there was zero chance my mom would go for it.

Cabbage shrugged. "It's more about the speech than what you bring."

I didn't exactly agree but didn't want to mention that I was worried about kids (Marni) judging me.

Also, it was at this moment that I realized I had no idea what sort of research my uncle was doing with Ludwig. So much for my being a good scientist and asking lots of questions.

Anyway, I still wasn't sure what to do. After all, the bar was set very high—at Labradoodle.

It was an awkward drive to the mall because Mom grilled me more about Marni and what she'd said and done. She wanted to be sure she got every single detail so she knew what to say to the principal. The more she talked about it, the more anxious I got about the whole thing. Taking it to the principal seemed so next-level. What would Marni do then? Did I really want to poke the bear? But there was no stopping my mother. I could only hope she knew what she was doing.

Mom needed some clothes for work, so once we got into the mall, we started at Walmart. After she tried on a million shirts just to find two she liked, we finally checked out.

"Can we go to the pet store now?" I asked.

Mom smiled at me. "We'll get there, but how about we stop at the nail place first and see if they can fit us in to get manis and pedis?"

I'd only been for a manicure and pedicure once, when Mom took my sister and me to the spa before Brandon and

Chloe's combined bar and bat mitzvah. I'd liked how they'd made my toes look so cute with colored polish. I'd tried to do my own since then, but they always turned out awful—better to leave it to the professionals, Mom liked to say. Normally I didn't care too much. But even so, I was looking forward to getting my nails painted. I was also happy that Chloe wasn't with us—this was special Mom-and-me time, something that almost never happened.

We got to the white and pink nail salon and were about to go in when I stopped in my tracks. Inside, sitting on the big pedicure chairs, were Marni and Shannon. They each had a lady working on their feet as they scrolled on their phones and talked at each other.

I shrunk into myself and fought the urge to run. At least they hadn't noticed me. Yet.

I can't go in there, I thought, my heart thudding hard in my chest.

"Arden?" Mom said, looking down at me with a frown. "You okay?"

I forced a smile on my face and turned away from the doorway so if one of the girls *did* happen to look over, she'd only see my back. "Oh, yeah, um…you know what? I'm really hungry—maybe even a little faint. Can we get lunch first? Like, now?" I didn't want to tell her about Marni and ruin our girls' day. Or, worse, risk having her say something to Marni right there at the mall. So awkward.

She blinked a few times and then nodded. "Yeah, sure. Okay."
Whew. Crisis averted!

It didn't take long to order and eat our food (KFC, even though it made me feel guilty to think it was chicken, which is a *bird*), so by the time we were sorting our recyclables from our trash, not a lot of time had passed since we'd left the salon. Despite my having stalled as much as I could, Marni and Shannon might still be in there.

"How about we go to the pet store first?" I suggested. "That way we won't mess up our nails before we even get home. We should definitely go to the salon last."

Mom nodded. "Good thinking," she said, putting her arm around me.

"Well, I *am* your smartest child—those other two have to share a brain," I said in my fake-snooty voice, making her laugh. I was joking, of course, but I did feel a little proud of how I'd come up with a good reason out of nowhere. And that it had worked.

But as we walked toward the pet store, something nagged at me. That something was the realization that even though I'd thought the thing with Marni was over because she'd gotten on the team, it wasn't. I was still scared of her. Just look at how I'd cowered from the salon. I would *always* be scared of her.

Unless I did something about it.

Sigh. Maybe Cabbage and Mom were right. Telling on her and getting help was the only way I'd ever get free of her.

But knowing this wasn't going to make it any less terrifying to go into the principal's office on Monday morning.

It had been only a few weeks since I'd been to the pet store, but it felt totally different this time. I had a *real* pet at home that I was buying for, not a maybe-someday-wished-for pet for which I made mental shopping lists but never actually bought anything. This was way more exciting. I was a real pet owner, or, at least, a temporary guardian, who had a legit reason to be here.

For the first time ever, I bypassed the dog and cat departments and went right to the bird area of the store. I stopped at Paco's cage. He growled, but I stood my ground.

"Hi, Paco," I said in a soft voice, the kind I used when talking to Ludwig. "I know you like to growl and lunge at people, but I bet you're only mean because people tease you. I get that now, and I'm sorry if people are awful."

Paco continued to growl. But I didn't take it personally this time. I felt more sorry for him than frightened now that I knew his behavior was a reaction to people treating him badly.

"Poor bird," Mom said.

"I know," I said. "Anyway, Paco, I hope you have a good rest of your day."

We left him and I led Mom over to the bird-food aisle.

"Does Ludwig need more pellets already?" Mom asked.

"Not yet," I said, thinking about how much I put in Ludwig's dish each day. He really didn't eat a lot (I was pretty sure he threw around more than he ate, based on how much I had to clean up off the floor), and Uncle Eli had brought over a big bag. "But that's the kind he eats," I added, pointing to the big bag of colorful pellets on the shelf.

"So what do you want to get him?"

I started down the aisle, past the perches and dishes to the toy section. I had never really looked at bird toys before, since I'd never considered a bird for a pet, thanks to Paco, but there were so many! Uncle Eli had told me it was a good idea to give Ludwig no more than two toys at a time. He'd said I should combine an indestructible puzzle toy made of hard plastic like his treat dispenser (to withstand his powerful beak) with a destructible one made of stuff like wood, paper, seashells and leather string (because birds *love* destroying things). I'd already seen how Ludwig had shredded one of his destructible toys, turning blocks of wood into basically tooth-picks and shavings at the bottom of his cage.

"Wow," Mom said, her eyes wide as she looked at all the rows of toys hanging on the display pegs. "There are so many. Who knew?"

"I know," I said, looking at the prices, too, because some of the toys were really expensive. One ginormous hanging toy was over forty dollars! "Maybe we'll just get one toy today— Uncle Eli did bring some over, after all."

"Good point," Mom said. "Why don't you pick out one toy and maybe…" She moved back down the row to where the food was. "How about something special for him to eat?"

I came up beside her and looked at all the bird treats, trying to figure out what Ludwig might like.

"What makes peanuts for birds special?" Mom asked, reaching for a bag of what looked like regular old peanuts in the shell.

"I don't know."

Mom flipped the bag over and looked at the back. "Probably just the price," she said with a snort. "This looks like thirty cents' worth of peanuts, and it's five bucks. Why don't you pick out a toy, and we'll go to the bulk store and get him some treats?"

I nodded and then, after thinking about it for a second, said, "Actually I should probably do some research first to see what foods are good for him. I read that you shouldn't give them certain people foods with added salt and other stuff. He has his almonds and mango pieces, so we can skip it for today."

Mom put her arm around me and gave me a squeeze. "You're so smart."

I smiled. "Smartest kid, remember?" Also, I hoped she saw what a responsible pet owner I was being. I was about to point it out when I heard someone say, "Hi, Claire, Arden."

We looked up, and there was Uncle Eli's friend, Simon, coming over to us. He was smiling, like he was really happy he'd run into us.

"Oh, hey, Simon," Mom said, her face lighting up. "What brings you here?"

He looked down at the bag of cat food under his arm. "Just doing some shopping."

"You have a cat?" I said, not realizing until the words were out of my mouth how ridiculous a question it was, because *obviously* he had a cat.

"Yep. Just me and Tesla at home. Tesla's my cat, in case that wasn't obvious," he added with a little chuckle as he pushed his glasses up with his free hand. He was acting so weird.

"Anyway," I said, pointing my thumb over my shoulder, "I'm going to go find a toy for Ludwig."

"Right!" Simon said, looking between Mom and me. "How's that going?"

"Fine," I said. "Great, actually."

"That's good," he said with a big smile. "Your uncle knows Ludwig's in good hands."

"Thanks," I said and then looked at Mom, because I didn't want to be rude, but—

"Go on," she said. Then she turned to Simon and said, "Heard from Eli?"

I waited, but Simon frowned and shook his head. "Not yet, no." Since he didn't have any news about my uncle, I left them to chat so I could return to finding Ludwig a toy.

A few minutes later I was still contemplating which one to get when I heard, said in the snottiest voice ever, "What are *you* doing here? *You* don't have a pet."

Marni and her sidekick, Shannon. After I thought I'd avoided them! I glanced in the other direction and saw my mom still busy talking to Simon and not paying me any attention. I wasn't about to call her over to protect me, but it was somewhat reassuring that she was right there, just in case.

"I'm talking to you, Arden!" Marni barked.

I thought about Cabbage and how he didn't let her bother him. Taking a deep breath, I looked at her and Shannon like I wasn't scared and said, "Getting a toy for my parrot."

She snorted. "A bird? How boring." Her eyes rolled so hard they almost disappeared in her head.

Cabbage would have ignored her, but I couldn't stop myself from saying, "He's not boring at all. He's an African Grey parrot, and he talks and is *super* smart."

For half a second I saw her snarky look falter, but then it was right back. "Birds aren't smart." She pointed to the other side of the store. "Look at Paco. All he does is screech and bite people."

Shannon spoke up. "Actually, I saw a video on YouTube where this bird could ask for what food he wanted and identify different things, like wood and keys and paper. It even knew colors."

Marni gave her an evil look, but Shannon just shrugged. "Sorry, but it's true."

"Whatever," Marni said with a toss of her hair. "They probably CGI'd the video. I don't believe it. And anyway, you can't play with a bird or go to a bird park. Dogs are the only pets that *really* matter. I'm sure you remember when I brought Prince—my adorable and super-smart Labradoodle—for my show-and-tell speech," she said. "*Everyone* loved him. He's smart, way smarter than some stupid bird."

It was true that everyone had loved Prince, but that didn't mean everyone loved *her*. Poor Prince, having to live with her.

"Come on," Shannon said, grabbing Marni's arm and tugging her toward the front of the store. "We need to get the bus or I'm going to be late."

Marni rolled her eyes and gave me an evil glare before she turned, and the two of them left the store.

My heart was pounding hard, but I'd survived. And even though I was still scared of Marni and her snark and threats, I felt pretty proud of myself.

FIFTEEN

When I'd finally found a toy for Ludwig (a woven piñata made of dried and colored palm leaves that he could tear apart with that beak of his), Mom was *still* talking to Simon. I didn't think she'd noticed me talking to anyone, so I didn't bother telling her about Marni.

She paid for the toy and we said goodbye to Simon, who checked out behind us.

"So are you and Simon a thing now?" I asked Mom on the way to the salon, waggling my eyebrows.

She did a double take at me. "What? No! Why would you ask that?"

I grinned. "Um, because I have eyes, and it looked like you two were flirting."

Mom actually blushed. Hilarious.

"Flirting? No. We were talking about your uncle. Anyway, I hardly have time for dating with you three kids and work and everything."

"Okay, whatever," I said, making a mental note to ask Uncle Eli about Simon's status. If I could ever get hold of him.

When we got home with the toy for Ludwig, me with fancy purple-painted nails, Mom went to start on laundry and I went to greet Ludwig.

I sat down at the dining-room table and opened my coloring book again, picking a new picture to color, this one of another mathematician—Emmy Noether. I was determined to finish the whole book by the time Uncle Eli returned from Guinea. Once I was done, I was going to pick the best picture and frame it for him as a gift for next Hanukkah.

As I colored, I thought about the smart parrot Shannon had seen on YouTube. Thanks to my research, I knew his name was Alex. The sad part was, he'd died, but he was still famous for all the research that a scientist, Dr. Pepperberg, had done with him and other birds like him. Shannon was right that Alex had been able to identify things by what they were made of and by color.

I looked at Ludwig. "Do you know colors?" I asked him.

He turned his head and stared at me with one eye.

After a few moments I grabbed my favorite purple marker— the one Cabbage had been spinning earlier—and returned my eyes to my page.

As I pulled the cap off the marker, Ludwig suddenly began to talk. "Green beans, yellow peppers, orange…oranges!"

I gasped. He was saying colors! Right after I'd asked him about them!

I stood up and walked over to his cage. "You *do* under-stand, don't you?"

He did his little tail-wagging dance, which could mean yes. Or no. Who knew?

I held my hand with its newly painted nails toward him. "What color are my fingernails?"

He bobbed his head and then said, "Eggplant, eighty-nine cents!"

Eggplants are kind of purple, which meant he seemed to understand, but I needed to make sure. *Question everything.*

"Ludwig, did you really know the right answer to that math equation I got wrong on my test? On the papers that were under your cage the first day you were here?"

"Thirty-four!" he said and then did his nodding-up-and-down dance, even lifting a foot in what I had to believe was an excited wave. "Thirty-four! Thirty-four! EEEEEEEEEEEEEEEE!"

I pressed my hands to my ears. "Ludwig!" I yelled. "You can't do the fire alarm! People will get mad, and I'll get in trouble!" And by *people*, I mostly meant Mr. Thompson.

He stopped.

"Whoa," I said. "You can read and do math and under-stand colors and...holy...this is huge. Does Uncle Eli know about this?"

He instantly stopped dancing. "Surprise!" he said, which I took to mean no, that my uncle didn't know about all this. I hadn't done a *ton* of research on African Greys, but nothing I'd read or watched on YouTube talked about anything like this.

Alex was smart, but he'd never solved math equations or read grocery flyers!

"I'm going to have to tell him. This. Is. *HUGE.*"

Ludwig bobbed up and down, and I couldn't help but think he was agreeing with me. And that he was excited about it too.

I didn't have an email account of my own, so I'd have to send him something from Mom's.

I went down the hall and found her in the small closet that held our laundry machines. She was bent over, sorting clothes and tossing all the dark items into the big washer. She looked up at me and smiled. "Your nails look so cute. I love that color on you."

"Thanks," I said. "Yours look…um…tidy." Because she's a dental hygienist, she doesn't like using polish on her fingers, even though she wears gloves when she sticks her hands in people's mouths. She did get her toenails done a dark red, but they were hidden in her slippers.

"What's going on?" she asked, raising her eyebrows.

"What do you mean?"

She tilted her head. "You're bouncing up and down like you're about to jump out of your skin. What's up, Arden?"

"Oh! Just…Ludwig did a funny trick. Can I use your email to send Uncle Eli a message?" I asked. "I want to tell him all about Ludwig and how he's doing."

"Sure," she said as she grabbed a pair of Brandon's jeans and checked the pockets, rolling her eyes at all the junk she pulled out (a pen, gum wrappers, coins).

She tossed the jeans in the washer before she stood up straight and let out a breath. "Tell him to give me a call when he gets a chance. Laptop's in my bag in the living room, so you'll have to boot it up."

I thanked her and took her laptop to the dining room. I sat at the table and opened it, looking over at Ludwig while I waited for the computer to boot up.

"Do you miss Uncle Eli?" I asked him.

He blinked at me a few times but didn't say anything.

When the laptop was ready, I clicked on the email icon and opened up the program. Uncle Eli was in her contacts, so I started a new message to him.

Hi, Uncle Eli, it's Arden, using Mom's email to contact you. I hope you are doing lots of great research in Guinea! Ludwig is doing great. He's been talking a little, but you said I should tell you if he does any strange things. I don't know if this is what you mean by strange, but he is so smart and he's been saying REALLY smart things. I don't know if you know who Alex the bird was, but I think Ludwig is even SMARTER!

I paused as I considered how to say, without sounding ridiculous, that I thought the bird understood me. I also didn't want to freak my uncle out.

Maybe we could talk about how smart he is and what he understands. I'm also thinking that maybe I should keep a journal of things he says that are intelligent. Write back soon! Miss you!

p.s. Mom wants you to call her when you can.
p.s.p.s. I think your friend Simon has a crush on her.
p.s.p.s.p.s. She might have one on him too.

As I stared down at the screen, I thought about telling him what had happened with the Science Bowl tryouts. Except that would make him sad, especially since the drama wasn't over. And it wasn't like he could do anything about it—he was half a world away! I didn't want him to worry.

Maybe I'd send him another message after we'd gone to the principal's office. Assuming it all went well, of course. Ugh, I didn't even want to think about it!

Putting thoughts of Monday out of my head, I read over my message and pressed the Send icon.

"There," I said to Ludwig. "I sent Uncle Eli a message because I need to talk to him about how smart you are. I told him you were doing okay, so he doesn't have to worry about you being taken care of."

Ludwig bobbed up and down but didn't say anything.

"Silly bird." I opened up my coloring book and reached for a blue marker.

"Now, Ludwig," the bird said a few minutes later, making me freeze in mid-color, "you're going to stay at my niece Arden's house. She's going to take good care of you while I'm gone."

I was speechless. Not only had he said what I was sure he'd heard my uncle say—which was amazing enough—but he'd also said it in a voice exactly like my uncle's! If my eyes had been closed, I would have thought Uncle Eli was in the room, speaking to the bird!

"Whoa," I said. "That is amazing!"

"Slam dunk!" Ludwig said and then did his little excited wiggling dance. We laughed together for a long time.

"Boy, I wish I could take you to show-and-tell," I said once our giggles had subsided. "That'd show Marni who has the best pet."

As I watched him, I wondered just how much he understood.

"Ludwig?" I said and watched as he turned one eye on me. "If I took you to school with me, would it freak you out?"

"Cool as a GREEN cucumber," Ludwig said.

"Does that mean you'd be cool and wouldn't mind?" I asked, thinking back to the day he'd arrived and how he'd bitten Uncle Eli when he was scared. What would stop him from doing that if I packed him up in his carrier and took him to school? I didn't know, but he seemed different now. Like he was Alex smart when he'd arrived but now was ten times smarter. Now he was *Ludwig* smart. "I don't want you to get upset." And I sure didn't want to get bitten.

"Arden's going to take gooooood care of you," he said.

It made my throat get tight, hearing my uncle's voice. "That means you trust me, right?" I asked.

"Signs point to YES!" he said, again in Uncle Eli's voice, and I recognized the phrase as one of the answers on the Magic 8 Ball my uncle had given me for my last birthday. He'd said it was one of his favorite toys from when he and Mom were kids. It was funny that he still played with one. With his bird.

But this was less important than what Ludwig had said, which, if I was interpreting correctly, was that he was okay with going to show-and-tell with me on Tuesday.

I did wonder why he was so chatty all of a sudden. It was like he'd turned on a switch and was making up for lost time since he'd arrived. Not that I was complaining. I had the smartest pet around. Labradoodles are nice and all—even Marni's Prince, I hated to admit—but Ludwig was *way* better than a Labradoodle.

I glanced toward the laundry closet, thinking that maybe I should ask Mom.

But then I realized she'd either say no, because she didn't understand that Ludwig *wanted* to go to school with me, or she'd say I could only take him if she came along. And with her already taking time off to talk to the principal, well, that wasn't going to happen.

I looked back at Ludwig. "I'll take you, but it'll just be our secret, okay?"

"Outlook good!" he said with a butt waggle. While Monday would be awful because of the Marni thing, I suddenly couldn't wait for Tuesday—my presentation was going to be amazing! All the kids were going to see that I had the coolest pet ever.

SIXTEEN

We were in the school's main office, sitting on the bench against the wall, waiting to be seen by the principal. Not only was I really, REALLY worried about what Marni was going to do after we told on her, but I also felt sick to my stomach because just being here in the office, waiting to talk to the principal, made me feel like *I'd* done something wrong.

I'd never been called to the office before (except for the time I forgot my lunch and Mom dropped it off, but that didn't count), and it felt weird. Bad. Scary. Wrong.

I swallowed and looked up at my mom, but she was busy scrolling on her phone. She didn't seem worried, but why would she? Marni couldn't hurt *her*. Mom had taken the morning off but was dressed in her scrubs and would go to work after the meeting with the principal.

Not that we had scheduled an official meeting. Mom had confidently marched up to the front desk and told the secretary, Mrs. Amberly, that we were there to see Ms. Cipriani about an important issue. Mrs. Amberly had nodded and picked up her phone, speaking into it so softly that we couldn't hear. Once she hung up, she told us to have a seat and Ms. Cipriani would be out shortly.

Mom must have finally noticed me looking at her, because she glanced down at me and smiled. "It's going to be fine, Arden," she said, her eyebrows scrunched up in her concerned-mom look. "Please don't be anxious. We'll get this all straightened out, okay?"

Her words didn't make me feel better, but her sudden side hug that gave me a fresh whiff of her nice shampoo did. Plus, the fact that she was there with me helped a little. So did knowing that Cabbage was down the hall in my classroom, which meant I had at least one friend who had my back. Brian too. And maybe Charlotte, but I wasn't positive she would stand up to Marni if it came to that.

Cabbage for sure, though.

Once we were done telling her about Marni, Ms. Cipriani sighed and pushed her glasses up onto the top of her head.

I'd told her everything, from how Marni had always called me a nerd (in a mean way) to how she had cornered and threatened me in the bathroom, how she'd made mean faces at me during the tryouts and even how I'd messed up the questions on purpose because of her. I'd also told her how Marni had dumped on the Science Bowl right up until Brian broke up with her and then had decided she needed to get on the team to impress him.

"I don't think she even cares about the Science Bowl," I'd said, still mad about how unfair it was that she had gotten on the team. "And it doesn't make sense that she did well at the tryouts."

"She must have studied," Ms. Cipriani had said with a frown. Like she didn't really believe it either.

I didn't have any proof of my hypothesis that Marni had cheated, but I hoped Ms. Cipriani would come to the same conclusion on her own. It almost felt like she was halfway there.

She pulled her glasses back down onto her face. I hadn't thought she was mad at me, but I still felt better when she looked right at me and said, "I'm very sorry you had to deal with this, Arden. What Marni did is unacceptable behavior, and we're going to have to meet with her and her parents. We don't take bullying lightly at this school."

"She didn't hit me or anything like that," I said.

"I'm glad that it never got physical," Ms. Cipriani said. "We have a zero-tolerance policy for violence here. But bullying includes threats and intimidation, and we don't excuse that kind of behavior just because it doesn't include physical violence. You should feel safe and supported coming to school."

The way she was looking at me, I knew she meant it and that I could add her to the list of people who had my back.

"Okay," I said, my voice squeaky but from relief. "Thank you."

She glanced at her computer, which was when Mom looked down at me and lifted her eyebrows as if to say, *See? I told you. It's going to be fine.*

I looked back at the principal and watched as she clicked her mouse a few times and then turned to Mom. "Tomorrow, early afternoon, work for you?"

Mom twisted her mouth and said, "I had to take this morning off already, so any chance we can do it after four?"

Ms. Cipriani squinted at her computer. "I'm available at four thirty."

"Fine," Mom said.

Ms. Cipriani nodded and scribbled something on a notepad. "Let me call Marni's parents to arrange it—hopefully they're available at that time, but I'll do what I can. Mrs. Amberly will call you later today to confirm."

"Thank you," Mom said.

I had a feeling the meeting was about to end. A weird, panicky feeling.

"But—" I started and then had to clear my throat. "I…I'm still…kind of…well, scared of her…I know I shouldn't be, but…what if…?" I huffed out a breath. This was hard to talk about, but what if Marni cornered me in the bathroom for being a tattler between now and the following afternoon?

"Arden," Ms. Cipriani said, her head tilting as she spoke in a kind, soft voice. I could tell right away she knew exactly what was wrong. "Once we're finished here, I'm going to speak with Marni directly. And while that should be enough to get her to leave you alone, no matter what happens, if you feel unsafe or threatened at all, speak with a teacher or come to the office immediately. Do you understand?"

I nodded but still felt a little unsure.

"How about," Mom said, "if Arden keeps her phone on her, with the office number programmed in?"

We weren't allowed to have phones in our classrooms. We had to leave them in our lockers, taking them out only for lunch and at the end of the day. I didn't think Ms. Cipriani was going to agree, but she nodded. "That's a good idea. Would that make you feel more secure, Arden?"

"Yes," I said. "Thank you." My shoulders relaxed a little.

"All right. You may keep your phone with you today and tomorrow. With the sound off," she added with a pointed look. "I will not have you interrupting class with a noisy phone or distracted playing games. Understand?"

I gave her a nod. "Yes, ma'am."

"Fine." She looked up at the clock on the wall and pushed back from her desk.

"Wait," I said. "What about Science Bowl?" Because this was when Ms. Cipriani was supposed to tell me I would get to replace Marni on the team.

Ms. Cipriani looked at me, then to my mother and then back to me again. "Pardon?"

"I would have gotten all my answers right," I said. "Marni only got four. I would have beaten her and gotten on the team."

Ms. Cipriani let out a sigh. "Why don't we table this until tomorrow, when we can all discuss it?"

My face got hot and my heart began to race. *But that's not fair!* I wanted to yell. *She shouldn't be on the team! I should be on the team!*

"But… but…" Angry tears filled my eyes.

Mom put a hand on my arm and gave me a squeeze as she spoke to Ms. Cipriani. "You're not going to let Marni continue on the team, are you?"

"Let's discuss this tomorrow," Ms. Cipriani said, her voice very businesslike, giving nothing away. "I need to talk to Marni, and then once we're all together, we'll discuss how to proceed. I'm sure you understand that I can't just make unilateral decisions without speaking with all involved parties, including Mr. Yan, since he's in charge of the teams and tryouts."

Mom huffed but said, "Of course."

There wasn't much else we could do, so we left the principal's office, and I let Mom walk me down the hall toward my homeroom. The bell had rung and class had started already, so the halls were empty, our footsteps echoing off the tiled walls.

"Give me your phone," Mom said. When I handed it to her, she programmed in the school's number and switched off the ringer. She handed it back, and I slipped it into my pocket, out of sight but within reach.

"If something happens," she said, and when my eyes went wide she quickly added, "*Not* that I think anything will, just *if* it does, and if you're not near a teacher, call the office here first— they are closer than I am."

I nodded. As we got to the door of the classroom, she bent down to give me a kiss on the cheek—thankfully, the door was closed. Marni would have laughed her butt off if she'd seen me get kissed by my mom.

"Try to have a good day," Mom said. "Call me if you need anything, okay? Leave a message if I don't answer."

When she was at work, Mom couldn't answer her phone if she had her hands in someone's mouth, doing a cleaning.

"Okay," I said. "Thanks."

She gave me a weird, slightly sad look before she nodded toward the door. "All right, you'd better go in."

I knocked and opened the door, taking a deep breath before I walked into the room. I handed Mr. Sanderson the excuse slip Mrs. Amberly had given me and took my seat, not looking at anyone. Not even Cabbage.

Three minutes later Marni got called to the office.

I slid my hand in my pocket to touch my phone, even though Mr. Sanderson was at the front of the room. For some reason it made me feel better knowing I had it. As Marni walked past my desk, I didn't look at her but just held my breath, feeling her angry molecules firing at me the whole time.

The longer Marni was out of class, the more nervous I got. I could barely focus on Mr. Sanderson teaching us…something…and almost couldn't peel my eyes off the door, waiting. A quick glance at the clock told me it had only been a few minutes, but each one felt like forever. Waiting is the worst!

But then Marni did finally come back. Her eyes were all red, and her cheeks were blotchy. She'd been crying. Ugh. That was probably going to make her even meaner. At least she didn't look at me. She just quickly made her way down the aisle and took her seat.

It was a good sign. But I still had the rest of the day to get through.

SEVENTEEN

I felt like a giant coward when I asked Charlotte if she had to use the bathroom right before lunch, but I didn't want to be alone in there in case Marni decided to follow me in. Even if Charlotte thought I was weird, her thinking that was better than me risking getting cornered by a now *very mad* and probably vengeful Meanie Marni who'd gotten into trouble because I'd tattled on her.

In the end the trip to the washroom was drama-free. Marni didn't even go in—she stood at her locker, talking to Shannon like we didn't even exist.

When we were finished, we joined Cabbage, Brian and Andy Fernandez—the Science Bowl team alternate member—in the cafeteria for lunch.

While I was relieved about the non-incident with Marni, I soon felt sad about the lunch situation, which turned into an unofficial Science Bowl study session. I couldn't blame them, since the first heat was in three weeks, but still.

Charlotte apologized when they realized I was sitting there all quiet. I tried to act like it was no big deal. But it was. I felt like an outsider who didn't belong. I was the only one at our table who wasn't on the team.

As everyone studied, I pulled out my phone and texted my mom to tell her the day had been okay so far and that Marni hadn't done anything to get back at me. Yet.

Mom didn't respond right away, which meant she was busy with work, so I put the phone away and ate my egg-salad sandwich in silence.

I quickly got tired of listening to everyone talking about the Science Bowl. *Really* tired. Maybe that made me not very nice, but I didn't feel like helping them study when I wasn't even on the team. I tuned out and inside my head worked on my show-and-tell presentation.

My speech had to be about five minutes long, and I had most of it planned already. I would start by talking about Ludwig and what kind of a bird he was, his age, what it said on his foot band and how long he might live. Then I would talk a little about Alex the famous African Grey and what he had learned—explaining how it wasn't just tricks but that he could identify objects, what they were made of and what color they were. He could ask for things he wanted too. His communications showed real understanding and knowledge.

I would tell the kids how he was famous because of all the studies Dr. Pepperberg had done with him on language and intelligence—he wasn't just a circus act but a smart bird who could communicate. Then I'd finish by trying to get Ludwig to laugh or say a few words.

While I was pretty sure Ludwig was smarter than Alex, I wanted to talk to my uncle before I told anyone about Ludwig and his amazing reading and math skills. My instincts told me I should keep it a secret, because the way he'd started talking with me was on a whole different level than how Alex had interacted with Dr. Pepperberg. Like, a groundbreaking-scientific-discovery level.

Something was *really* different about Ludwig. But before I told the world about him, I wanted to know what my uncle knew and why Ludwig was so special.

Cabbage and I walked home from school together. It was the first time he'd had a chance to ask me about the meeting with the principal. I told him it had gone fine except for the part about how Mom and I had to meet with Marni and her family the next day. Oh, and the Science Bowl, of course.

"Maybe they'll let you try out again," he said.

"They should just let me in," I moaned. "Everyone knows I'm smarter than her. They should kick her off the team and just put me on. It's not fair."

When he didn't agree with me right away, I looked over at him. He had a weird look on his face.

"What?"

He shrugged. "Well, she did get four answers right. Same as what I got."

I rolled my eyes. "I don't believe she knew those answers." When Cabbage's eyebrows went up, I told him my hypothesis, that she had cheated.

He seemed to think about that for a minute, then shrugged. "But even if we had a way to find evidence, it wouldn't be enough. If they kick her off the team, they can't just put you on. That wouldn't be fair to Andy."

I realized that was true. Although I knew I could beat Andy too.

"Maybe they'll have to do all the tryouts again," he said. "To make it fair for everyone."

"Anyway," I said, suddenly not wanting to talk about it anymore, "can you come over after dinner so I can practice my speech on you?"

He nodded. "What does your mom think of you taking Ludwig to school?"

I made a face. "Well, I haven't exactly told her."

Cabbage didn't say anything but gave me a look that said, *Are you sure she'll be okay with that?*

"It's fine," I said, answering his unspoken question. "I'll take him and then bring him home at lunch. I'll have time to run him home if I hurry."

He stared at me some more, making me squirm. Cabbage could be so judgy sometimes.

"Okay, fine!" I said. "I'll tell her." *After*, I didn't say out loud. "So are you coming over tonight or what?"

"Yeah," he said. "Ludwig's cool."

I agreed. Although Cabbage didn't know just *how* cool.

EIGHTEEN

The next morning I got up early to check Mom's email, but there was nothing from Uncle Eli yet. I was eating my Cheerios at the dining-room table, chatting at Ludwig, when Mom left for work, promising me she'd pick me up downstairs right at four fifteen for the dreaded meeting.

Cabbage knocked on my door a few minutes before it was time to leave. "My mom's almost ready," he said as he followed me back inside, his backpack over his shoulders.

The night before, while Mom was with Brandon at hockey practice, and Chloe was in our room, doing whatever, I'd run through my presentation a bunch of times with Cabbage as my audience. It had reminded me that Ludwig didn't like to talk in front of strangers—all he'd done was stare at Cabbage. Still, Cabbage had said my presentation was good, even without the bird speaking. Having Ludwig there was a big enough deal, he'd assured me.

After that I'd begun to assemble all the stuff I needed to

take with me to show-and-tell. Cabbage offered to ask his mom if she could drive us to school. I thanked him and was relieved when Mrs. Devi said she would be happy to. I was really glad I wouldn't have to carry Ludwig and his stuff all the way.

Unlike my mom, who worked at a dentist's office, Mrs. Devi worked at home as a web designer, which meant she could work whenever she had to. Cabbage said some days she'd work in the middle of the night, until almost dawn, and other days she wouldn't work at all and might go out to see movies during the day. Mr. Devi, an accountant, worked regular days at an office.

"I need to pack up Ludwig," I said as I led Cabbage to the dining room. As I got out the carrier, I was suddenly worried that the bird wouldn't go in. Worried he'd bite me. Worried my presentation was going to be awful. Worried that Marni was going to—

"You okay, Arden?" Cabbage asked, breaking into my thoughts. I looked up, and he was standing there, looking at me funny.

"Yeah, why?" I asked, surprised to hear my voice was a little screechy.

"You seem…I don't know…frazzled."

I *was* frazzled. Not only was I starting to question if taking Ludwig to school was a good idea (and thinking just how mad Mom was going to be if she found out I'd taken Uncle Eli's important research-animal-slash-pet to school), but I also had the meeting with Marni and her parents to worry about.

At that moment I had no words to say any of this, and I just blinked at Cabbage as my mind whirled around at a million miles an hour.

"All right," he said, eyes wide. "So *that's* an alarming face. You okay?"

"No," I said as tears pricked my eyes, and I got really worried I was about to lose it. "I'm not okay. I'm…I'm sort of freaking out here."

He came over and tilted his head down, looking straight into my eyes as his black hair flopped over his forehead. "It's going to be okay, Arden. You'll nail your presentation, and then the meeting will be fine. You did nothing wrong—you're only going to be there to work it out. She can't hurt you."

"Tell that to my stomach," I said, pressing my hand to my belly because it felt like my Cheerios wanted out.

Cabbage smirked. "Come on. Let's pack up Ludwig."

I took a couple of deep breaths. "Okay, Ludwig," I said in my singsongy voice, hoping to get him excited about the day to come and maybe calm my own nerves by acting like everything was okay. "I hope you remember about your super-fun, cool adventure today! We're going to school!"

Ludwig looked from me to Cabbage and then back to me. It was hard to tell what he was thinking. I really wished he would talk to me so I could know if he was still into going to show-and-tell, but I knew there was no way he would with Cabbage standing right there.

Suddenly I got an idea. "Oh hey, Cabbage, can you go down to my bedroom and grab my backpack? Chloe and

Brandon are gone already, so you won't run into either of them."

"Sure," he said and left the room.

"Take your time," I called out before I quickly turned to the bird. "Okay, Ludwig, we only have a second, but are you absolutely sure you want to go to school with me today?"

"Cool for school! Slam dunk. Surprise!"

"Does that mean yes?" I asked. "Boy, I wish I could get a straight answer out of you."

"X-axis!" he said. It took me a minute to figure out an x-axis is the *straight* line at the bottom of a graph. That was his *straight* answer. What a bird!

"What's so funny?" Cabbage asked a second later as he came in with my backpack.

"Ludwig made a joke. A math joke!"

Cabbage's face fell as he looked between me and the bird. "And I missed it!"

"Sorry," I said. "He only just started talking in front of me. I'm sure he'll warm up to you soon."

"What kind of math joke?"

I recounted what Ludwig had said, laughing.

Cabbage didn't laugh. He had to have gotten it, though. "What's wrong?" I asked.

"If..." He shook his head like he was working something out. "If he said that...are you telling me...? Arden, are you having *actual* conversations with him that aren't just tricks you've taught him?"

"I haven't taught him anything." Excitement bubbled up

in me, and I nodded hard until I almost got dizzy. I loved that Cabbage was catching on to how smart Ludwig was—it made me feel like I wasn't just imagining it. "He really understands things."

"Since when?"

"I don't know. I haven't had a chance to talk to Uncle Eli yet, but I think only since he's been here, otherwise he definitely would have mentioned it before he left, right? I didn't catch on that he was understanding me until he really started talking. But the first clue was my math test. He figured out the answer that I got wrong."

Cabbage stared at me. "Wait, is that the one you called me about?"

"THIRTY-FOUR!" Ludwig said just then.

Cabbage's body froze, but his eyes went so wide they almost looked like they were going to pop out of his head. "Arden, this is…Ludwig can *read*? Whoa."

"I know," I said. "But I think we have to keep it a secret until I talk to Uncle Eli. There's something weird about all of this. I mean, Alex was smart, but—"

"Not like this," Cabbage said. He'd watched the Alex videos too. "What's your hypothesis?"

I laughed. "I have no idea. I've been observing, but none of it makes sense. I've been collecting lots of evidence, though."

Cabbage nodded. "Yeah, maybe a good idea to keep this quiet for now in case…" He paused. "What is your uncle's research?"

"I don't know," I said, exasperated. "That's why I've been trying to get hold of him. It's killing me that he's gone completely off-grid."

"Does your mom know?"

"No," I said.

He looked at me sideways. "Does she know you're taking him to school?"

"Errr...not yet," I said with a goofy smile.

"Surprise!" Ludwig said, making me snort. "Cool for school!"

Cabbage laughed. "Sounds like he wants to go. But what if he starts talking and solving math problems that are on the board or, I don't know, reciting Shakespeare?"

I turned toward the bird. "Do you even know Shakespeare?"

"To be or not to be...LUDWIG!" the bird yelled and then laughed.

Cabbage shook his head, looking conflicted. "I don't know if you should take him. What if he starts talking like this? How will you explain it? What would your uncle say?"

"He won't say anything," I said. "He's shy in front of strangers, remember?"

Cabbage seemed to think about that for a minute before he said, "All right. We'd better get him in his carrier. Mom will be here in a few minutes."

"Okay." I turned toward the table and opened the door to Ludwig's carrier. "You're not going to bite me, are you, Ludwig? If you want to have fun school adventures and impress all the kids, you need to get in the carrier." I opened the door of his cage and put my hand in—confidently—with the side of it just in front of him.

"Step up," he said before I got the chance to.

And then he did, his little feet gripping my fingers.

Thankfully, zero bites later, he was in his crate and we were on our way.

NINETEEN

Mrs. Devi wished me good luck and leaned over to give Cabbage a kiss before we collected our things and headed into the school. I carried Ludwig and his bag of stuff, and Cabbage was in charge of our backpacks. As we walked toward the entrance, I was suddenly reminded about my nervous bladder. And the huge glass of juice and the cereal milk I'd had at breakfast. Good thing we were still early.

"I need to use the bathroom," I said as Cabbage held the door open for me.

"Why don't you put him in the classroom. I'll…" He trailed off as he looked down. "Oh shoot. I grabbed your backpack but not mine." And then, before I could say anything, he pulled out his phone at the same time as he ran back toward the parking lot.

"Yes, Cabbage, I'll be fine," I said to no one as I shook my head and walked toward our homeroom. The door was open, but there was no one else there yet, which was something of a relief. I put Ludwig's carrier and the bag of his stuff on the back shelf of the classroom, next to a bunch of geography textbooks and out of the way. That way I could run to the bathroom, and if anyone came into the room, they probably wouldn't even notice him before I got back.

I bent down and looked through a hole in the carrier to see one eye staring back at me. "I'll be right back, Ludwig," I said. "Stay quiet until I return, okay?"

He didn't say anything, so I took that as agreement, left the classroom and jogged down the hall toward the bathroom.

Even though I hurried, by the time I got back, the classroom wasn't empty. I burst through the doorway, breathing hard because I'd run the whole way, and immediately stopped in my tracks when I saw Shannon and Marni standing right next to Ludwig's carrier. I almost had a heart attack, but then I realized they were just hanging out there talking, absorbed in their conversation. Maybe I was being paranoid, but the way they were standing so close together gave me the feeling they were talking about me.

Cabbage was sitting at his desk, facing the front of the room. He looked up as I arrived. "Hey," he said. "Sorry about that—I wanted to catch my mom before she got very far."

I went right over to him and nodded toward Marni and Shannon. "How long have they been here?"

He turned around and looked at the girls. "They were already here when I came in a second ago." He looked down at my empty hands. "Where's Ludwig?"

I pointed my chin toward the back of the room and quietly said, "Right behind them on the shelf. I don't think they—"

I was interrupted when Ludwig suddenly let out a super-loud growl, making Shannon and Marni jump and then scream like they were being murdered.

This made Ludwig growl louder. Then, all of a sudden, he started doing the fire alarm. At full volume!

"EEEEEEEEEEEEEEEEEEEEEEEE!!!!!!!!!!!!!!!!!!!!!!!!!!!!!"

"WHAT IS GOING ON?" Marni screamed as she and Shannon ran away from him, their palms pressed over their ears.

Even though it felt like my eardrums were shattering too, I hurried toward the back of the room to get to Ludwig. "Shhhhhh, Ludwig," I said in as calm a voice as I could, putting my face in front of the wire-mesh door of the carrier. He finally stopped doing the alarm, although he growled a little, but I knew it wasn't at me. He was probably just winding down from whatever had freaked him out. His feathers were all fluffed up, and the whites of his eyes were huge, which meant he was angry. Or stressed. Or something. I didn't know what he was feeling, but I did know it wasn't good.

"It's okay, Ludwig, don't worry. I'm back. Shhhhhhh. It's okay." I kept speaking, trying to soothe him. "I'm here. No one's going to hurt you."

Finally he must have believed me. He did a little shake, and then his feathers all lay flat on his body. He looked at me, his eyes back to normal. He bowed his head and stuck it against the bars. I reached out and scratched his feathers, still cooing at him to reassure him that everything was all right.

"What happened?" Cabbage asked in a low voice beside me.

I looked at him. "I don't think the girls actually did anything," I said, "because I was watching them when Ludwig started freaking out. I think he just got spooked by them standing there. Maybe they were too close. He's so sensitive. But he seems okay now. Aren't you, Ludwig?"

"What is *in* there?" Marni demanded all of a sudden.

As I turned around, I noticed she'd kept a good distance between her and me, which I was sure had everything to do with Ludwig.

"My parrot," I said. "Ludwig. He's the topic of my presentation today."

She stared at me for a long moment and then burst into laughter. "Right. Because that screeching thing is just as cool as a *dog*."

Instantly mad, I opened my mouth to defend Ludwig, but Cabbage spoke before I got the chance.

"Marni, no one asked for your opinion. Just go sit down."

It looked like she was about to say something else, but instead she narrowed her eyes at Cabbage, shut her mouth and turned around, walking off to take her seat.

"How do you do that?" I asked.

Cabbage looked at me with his curious face. "Do what?"

"Not let her get to you."

"I just don't." He shrugged. "Do you *really* care what she thinks?"

"I—" I stopped, because I realized in that second that I actually *didn't* care what she thought. I mean, I always had before, but maybe only because she had convinced me that I *should*. But did I really need her to think Ludwig was cool to make *me* believe he was? No. I *knew* Ludwig was cool and smart and WAY better than her dog. "Huh," I said. "I guess I don't care. It seems so ridiculous now that I *would*."

"Don't beat yourself up," Cabbage said. "My mom said people like her act like they do to make you think what they say matters. But only because they feel bad about themselves. They tear other people down to make themselves feel better."

Was that why she was so mean? Had Brian asking her why she couldn't be more like me made her so mad because she felt bad about herself?

As if a light bulb had turned on in my head, I suddenly saw her differently. And I knew, in that moment, that I'd never be scared of her again.

"I get it now," I said to Cabbage. "I totally get it."

I glanced over at her. When she caught my look and glared back, I just smiled. It was strange—and amazing—not to feel intimidated.

"Good morning, everyone!" Mr. Sanderson said as he came into the room, causing us to turn around and face him. As more kids came in behind him and took their seats, he leaned down and put his briefcase beside his desk. Then he glanced up at the clock and said, "We've got about four minutes until the bell, but we have several speeches today, so I want to start on time."

He smiled and looked around the classroom. "We're going to start with Charlotte and then Fiona, Arden, Sam and George," he said, looking at us in turn as he called our names.

That meant my presentation would be right in the middle, and I suddenly understood why Brian had wanted to go first at the Science Bowl.

I used those last four minutes to run to the bathroom again. Stupid nervous bladder!

TWENTY

It's only five minutes, it's only five minutes, I told myself as Fiona presented her speech about her family's trip to New Zealand, complete with a slideshow of blown-up pictures. Normally I would have been attentive, as New Zealand did look like a beautiful and interesting place, but I was way too distracted by worrying about my own speech.

Before I knew it, her five minutes were up and it was my turn.

I got up out of my seat. On my way back to collect Ludwig, Cabbage caught my eye. "Need help?" he asked.

"I'm okay, thanks," I said to him as I passed by. I carefully grabbed Ludwig's carrier with one hand and the bag of stuff with my other, taking it with me to the front of the room.

Just five minutes. You got this, Arden. I chanted it over and over inside my head.

Mr. Sanderson watched me with a curious smile as I put the carrier on his desk and got out my items to pass around—a little sandwich bag filled with bird food and the big feather that I'd found on the bottom of Ludwig's cage two days earlier. I also took out my handout pages, which I put down on the corner of Mr. Sanderson's desk.

"Hi, um, so my speech is on African Grey parrots. And I brought with me Ludwig, who is my uncle's parrot that I'm taking care of while he's on sabbatical—which is a research trip." I turned toward the carrier, praying silently that Ludwig wouldn't suddenly decide to get cranky.

"Marni," Mr. Sanderson said. "We're going to wait for Arden to finish before we have questions."

Sure enough, Marni's hand was up, and she looked like she was going to launch out of her seat.

"But Mr. Sanderson, that thing growled at me before. I don't think it should come out of the cage if it's dangerous."

I looked at the teacher, who then turned to me. "Arden?"

"He's not dangerous, Mr. Sanderson. He's really sensitive and shy around strangers, so he was probably just nervous when she got too close to his cage."

"It's going to fly at me and peck my eyes out!" Marni said, and either she was a better actor than I'd have guessed or she really was scared.

"He's not going to peck your eyes out," I said, trying not to picture Ludwig doing just that.

"I know about birds! There's that one at the pet store—"

"He's not like Paco," I said and then turned to the teacher. "His wings are clipped, so he can't fly. And I was just going to take him out to show everyone. I will hold him on my hand,

and as long as no one gets too close, I'm sure he'll be fine." *I hope.*

"His wings are clipped?" Mr. Sanderson asked.

"Yes, sir."

He looked at Marni. "Well, I feel pretty safe. If the bird can't fly, there isn't much chance that he can peck your eyes out from across the room."

Marni huffed but didn't say anything.

When the teacher nodded at me, I opened the door to the carrier. "All right, Ludwig," I said in my calm voice. "It's showtime, but all you have to do is look pretty, okay?"

I was fairly sure he could understand what I was saying, but the most important thing I was trying to communicate was calmness, how I wanted *him* to stay calm and not freak out or growl at anyone (even if certain people probably deserved it).

I put my hand in, holding my breath, and then said confidently, "Step up."

He did, his little feet gripping the side of my hand, and I pulled him out and lifted my arm so everyone could see. He did one of his little feather fluffs.

Excited chatters went around the room. I just hoped all the voices wouldn't freak him out.

"Now, everyone," Mr. Sanderson said, "please keep your voices down. Arden has her speech to do, and we don't want to scare the bird."

"Thank you," I said. I took a deep breath and looked at Cabbage, who did a thumbs-up, giving me a boost of confidence.

"So this is Ludwig, and he's my uncle's African Grey parrot. African Grey is the common name for two species of parrots, Congo (*Psittacus erithacus*) and the smaller Timneh (*Psittacus timneh*). Ludwig is a Timneh, characterized by his darker feathers and more maroon tail."

I turned him a little so everyone could see his dark-red tail feathers.

"Greys come from Africa, obviously, particularly the western side of the continent—Guinea, Congo and Ghana, among other countries. Ludwig was hatched here in captivity and raised by a breeder, like dogs and cats, and he even has a band on his foot with his hatch date and breeder code."

Just then, as if I'd trained him to, Ludwig lifted his ringed foot.

Everyone laughed. There was also a chorus of "Whoa" and "Cool!"

"Good job, Ludwig," I said.

Encouraged by how interested everyone seemed to be, I continued my speech.

"Greys are known for their ability to speak and mimic not just the human voice but many different sounds, especially the ones they think are interesting. For example"—I laughed a little—"if you were here before class, you might have heard him do the fire alarm."

"That's what that was!" Mr. Sanderson said. "We couldn't figure it out down in the teachers' lounge, but by the time we got up to investigate, it was done." He chuckled.

I nodded. "He also does the microwave."

As if on cue, Ludwig—who I'd never expected would speak at all in front of such a big group of strangers—did the *ker-chunk…beep, beep, beep…hmmmmmm, hmmmmm.*

Everyone laughed as they recognized the sound.

"What else does he do?" Andy said excitedly, not bothering to put up his hand.

"Don't forget," Mr. Sanderson said. "We're going to keep questions for the end." Then he looked at the bird and added, "You too, Ludwig. Let Arden finish."

Ludwig did a little bobbing dance on my finger, making everyone laugh.

"Anyway, I also wanted to talk about the research that Dr. Irene Pepperberg has done. She had an African Grey named Alex…"

I went on and spoke about Dr. Pepperberg's famous research with Alex and other birds, which determined that birds are as smart (and sometimes as crabby) as two-year-old humans. I could tell the class was really interested in what I was talking about by the way they all watched me and Ludwig the whole time.

Once I got to the end of what I wanted to say, I felt good, *really* good, about how it had gone and even looked forward to answering some questions.

"So that's all of my speech," I said. "But there's a lot of information about Alex and Dr. Pepperberg's research online, and I've put a bunch of links on my handout, including some to YouTube videos where you can see him and some other research birds. Thank you."

As everyone clapped, I handed the stack of pages to Charlotte at the front of her row for her to pass out, along with the bag of pellets and the feather.

"I can answer some questions now," I said, suddenly hoping there wouldn't be too many as my arm was getting tired from holding Ludwig up for so long.

A bunch of hands went up. "Shannon?" Mr. Sanderson said. "You're up first."

Shannon opened her mouth to speak, but before even one word came out, Ludwig began to speak. In Shannon's exact voice. "Do they know you stole the Science Bowl questions? Is that what the meeting is about?"

The entire room gasped. Everyone had already been looking at the bird, but now all sets of eyes in the room were laser focused on him. Especially mine.

"What?" I whispered.

Ludwig went on, but this time in Marni's voice. "No, no one knows I took them. Everyone thinks I'm just really smart. The meeting's because they say I bullied Arden into getting all her answers wrong."

Everyone turned and stared at Marni. But Ludwig wasn't done. Back in Shannon's voice, he said, "Well, you kind of did bully her, didn't you?"

At that point, Marni—the *real* Marni—spoke up. "Mr. Sanderson! Arden taught her bird to say all those lies. None of it is true!"

Of course, I hadn't—even if I'd wanted to, how could I teach the bird to speak in the girls' voices so perfectly?

I turned to the teacher. "I didn't, I promise. I don't even know how..."

Then I remembered Shannon and Marni whispering in front of Ludwig's carrier before class started. They must have had that very conversation.

I looked at Ludwig, and I could have sworn he gave me a knowing glance. "I'm putting you away," I said, unable to focus on him while all this drama was unfolding around me. I bent down to put him in his carrier and closed the door.

"Marni, Shannon," Mr. Sanderson said in a stern voice. "I'd like to see you out in the hall."

Those girls were so busted.

Looking like they were being called to their doom, Marni and Shannon got up from their chairs and followed the teacher out of the room.

Once the three of them were gone and the teacher had pulled the door closed, the class erupted in chatter, everyone talking about what had just happened. As I took Ludwig's carrier to the back of the class again so he could settle down, Cabbage came to my side.

"What was that?" he said, his eyes wide.

I looked over my shoulder to see Charlotte coming over. "Is that true?" she asked. "Did she steal the Science Bowl questions?

"I don't know." I shrugged. "But I had hypothesized that she must have cheated."

"It would explain how she did so well," Cabbage said.

Charlotte nodded. "I was thinking the same thing."

"It's the only explanation that makes any sense," I said. "She's never done well in science, and I don't think she could have been lucky enough to get so many questions right."

"Ludwig must have heard them talking," Cabbage said, coming to the same conclusion I had. "I wonder if the teacher will believe it, though."

We all looked toward the door, although of course we couldn't see into the hallway.

"Anyway," Charlotte said, turning back to look at me, "your speech was awesome. I never knew how smart birds could be!"

"Ludwig did a good job," I said, proud of how Ludwig had impressed everyone *and* made them laugh.

"Ludwig did a good job," Cabbage agreed. Then he leaned in close and bumped my shoulder with his. "But you did a *great* one."

Mr. Sanderson returned about five minutes later, a serious look on his face. That he was alone was alarming.

Cabbage and I looked at each other questioningly and then returned to our seats after I'd said a quick "Be good" to Ludwig.

"All right," Mr. Sanderson said. "We should carry on with our speeches. Who is next?" It was as though nothing had happened. But what did it mean? Where had Shannon and Marni gone?

Sam went to the front of the room with his maps and globe and started his speech about climate change, but I was too distracted to pay attention. I was too busy thinking about what Ludwig had said. Or, more accurately, what Ludwig had *repeated*.

It had to be true, right? Did birds know how to lie? Did they have the imagination to make up stuff?

Even if they did, it made more sense to me that what he'd blurted out was true. Based on my observations, Marni was the one most likely to lie and cheat. And she had been so busted. By a bird.

I almost—*almost*—felt sorry for her.

TWENTY-ONE

Shannon came back to class before lunch, but Marni didn't. I didn't have the guts to ask Shannon what had happened, so where Marni had disappeared to remained a mystery for the rest of the school day. Had she been suspended? Sent home? Was she sitting in the principal's office? Had she run away from the school?

I'd find out soon enough.

Luckily I was kept pretty occupied for the rest of the day. It had been a busy morning of kids constantly wanting to see and learn more about Ludwig, which I thought was great. But it got a little tiring. Thankfully, that ended at lunchtime, when Cabbage called his mom and she came to get us so we could take Ludwig home. The afternoon went by in a flash—maybe because I was dreading the meeting with the principal.

After school I sat at the dining-room table, doing home-work, until Mom texted. She was leaving work, and I was to come down and meet her. So yeah, whatever had happened to Marni, the meeting was still on.

I said a soft goodbye to Ludwig, but he was sleeping, standing on one foot, his beak tucked into the feathers around his back. I rushed out the door to the elevator, trying to figure out how this meeting was going to go down. Marni was definitely in trouble—at least for one and now maybe two things. But what did that mean for me? Was I on the team? Was I in trouble for something I didn't even know about? I hated not knowing.

If Marni had stolen the Science Bowl tryout answers—which the evidence suggested—she'd get kicked off the team for sure. But would the principal believe that *a bird* had known the truth when he'd tattled on her?

I snorted. A *bird* as our prime witness! I couldn't wait to tell my uncle about this. As I rode down in the elevator, my heart ached a little just thinking about Uncle Eli. He still hadn't emailed back, and I *really* needed to talk to him. Especially now.

I got down to the lobby just as Mom was pulling up to the curb, so I went through both sets of doors and jumped into the front seat.

"How did it go today?" she asked while I buckled in.

"My speech went really well. I didn't mess up, and all the kids seemed to be interested in Lud—" That's when I remembered that I hadn't told her I'd taken the bird to school.

Mom was pulling away, but she glanced over at me for a second. "What? What are you talking about? I was asking how your day was with that girl. She didn't do anything, did she?"

Oh.

"Oh. No, that was…I mean, Marni was…she didn't do anything to me today. Not exactly."

Mom took her eyes off the road briefly to shoot me a confused look. "Arden, what's going on?"

Sigh. She was going to find out. I'd get in a lot less trouble if she heard it from me. I'd learned that lesson in the past. The hard way.

"I…so I took Ludwig to school today."

"What?" She slammed on the brakes, making me thankful I was buckled in.

"Please don't get in an accident!" I yelled, but she'd already started moving again when the car behind us honked.

"Sorry," she said, waving apologetically in her rearview mirror before she glanced at me for a second. "You did what?"

"I took Ludwig to school for my show-and-tell speech," I said, cringing. But then I quickly added, "And it went really well! I bet I'll get an A, and he didn't bite me or anyone else. Did I mention I'll probably get an A?"

She breathed out loudly through her nose, keeping her eyes on the road. "You should have asked first, Arden."

"I was scared you would say no unless you were there and, well, you're really busy with work all the time, and I wouldn't have gotten to do such a great presentation."

She glanced over at me and then sighed as she turned her eyes back to the road. "You're probably right that I would have said no. And I can't afford the time off—you're right about that too, Arden. I wish that wasn't so, but it is."

"I know. But having him there was awesome. All the other kids and even Mr. Sanderson were really interested. Ludwig even did the microwave thing."

She smiled and then pressed her lips together, like she didn't want to smile because she was supposed to be mad.

"You…" She sighed. "Arden, he's not your bird, just your responsibility. And he's not even simply a pet either—he's your uncle's research animal. You need to be really careful with him."

"I know, and I was," I assured her. "I took him in his carrier, and Mrs. Devi drove me and Cabbage to school and picked us up at lunch so we could bring him home. We figured it was enough excitement for him just to be there for the morning."

She nodded. "That was a good decision, and I'm glad Henri's mom drove you. Still, you should have asked me." She paused, glancing again at me. "But since you were *mostly* responsible about it, I'll let it go this time. Next time let's talk about it first, all right?"

"Deal," I said, relieved that she seemed okay with it in the end and I wasn't going to be punished.

"Okay, so," she said with another sigh, "anything else new that I need to know before this meeting?"

"Kind of," I said when she prodded me with one of her mom looks. I bit my lip, not sure how to tell her the rest of what had happened.

"Well?" She raised her eyebrows.

I took a deep breath and filled her in on how Ludwig had totally busted Marni.

When we got to the school office, it was only twenty-five after four, so we weren't late. But it felt like we were when Mrs. Amberly waved toward the principal's closed door and said, "Go right in. They're waiting for you."

Mom gave me an encouraging smile before she knocked on the door twice and then turned the handle.

"Come in," Ms. Cipriani said, getting up from her seat and gesturing toward the two empty chairs. There were only two because the rest were filled by Marni and the two people I assumed were her parents based on the fact that they were adults. And on how unhappy they looked.

A quick glance at Marni's scowling face told me she was even more unhappy. More unhappy than usual, I mean.

Good, a little part of me said as I sat down, even though I knew it was mean.

"Thank you for coming," Ms. Cipriani said, as though we were doing her a favor. She sat back down behind her big desk and let out a loud breath before she started speaking again. "I called this meeting to talk about what happened around the Science Bowl tryouts, but based on some other information that has been brought to my attention, I asked the Olsens to come in at four o'clock so I could discuss all of this with them first."

Between that and Marni's scowling face, I knew this meant they were taking Ludwig's "evidence" seriously. I wanted to do a fist pump but knew it wouldn't go over well, so I did a mental one inside my head.

"All right," Mom said, folding her hands in her lap.

Instead of saying more, the principal looked pointedly at Marni, but she had her head down. She must have felt everyone's eyes on her, because she fidgeted a little.

"I believe you have something to say," Marni's mom said impatiently, poking her daughter's arm with a finger.

Marni fidgeted some more and then huffed loudly before she said, "I shouldn't have been mean to you at the Science Bowl tryouts."

I waited for more, but the only sound in the room for several long seconds (eight—I counted) was Ms. Cipriani's ticking clock.

That's it? That's her apology?

"And?" her mother prompted with another poke, poke.

Marni muttered something that sounded like "Mmm morry."

"What was that, young lady?" her father asked in a sharp tone.

"I said, 'I'm sorry,'" Marni blurted out. It wasn't very sincere or nice, but I figured it was the best apology I was going to get. I didn't really care as long as she left me alone.

Ms. Cipriani let out another loud breath before she turned to me and said, "Marni has taken full responsibility for her actions around the Science Bowl tryouts, from her attempts at manipulation and intimidation to—"

"*Attempts* at manipulation and intimidation?" Mom interrupted, sitting forward in her chair as she looked angrily from Ms. Cipriani to Marni and back. "I don't think she *attempted* anything. I think she *accomplished*. Arden deliberately threw her tryout because she was terrified."

I had never loved my mom as much as I did in that moment.

"You're right," Mrs. Olsen said, nodding. "And we have spoken to Marni about her behavior. She has assured us that she will not act that way in future toward Arden or anyone else. And for what it's worth, she will be punished at home."

"Additionally she will be given detention here at school," Ms. Cipriani added.

Mom turned to Mrs. Olsen, and her angry face melted a little as she nodded her head. "Thank you."

Ms. Cipriani adjusted her glasses and cleared her throat. "As I was saying, Marni has taken responsibility for her behavior, and I believe she understands why it was wrong. For that and other reasons, she will not be participating in the Science Bowl."

I did another mental fist pump.

"Does that mean Arden is on the team?" Mama Bear—I mean, *Mom*—asked.

"Despite her assurances that she knew all her answers, it wouldn't be fair to the other participants to simply put her on the team. Other students tried out and didn't make the cut."

I gasped, and Mom put her hand on my arm before I could yell out that it wasn't fair.

"But that doesn't mean you won't have another opportunity," the principal said, looking at me. "We'll be redoing tryouts for the seventh graders."

Mom nodded. "That seems fair," she said, rubbing my arm. I knew she was right, and it was what Cabbage had thought they'd do, so I wasn't totally surprised. But it wasn't exactly what I had hoped for. It had been stressful enough doing the tryouts once!

Still, as long as Marni wasn't there, I'd probably ace it.

"If there's nothing else?" Mom asked Ms. Cipriani.

"No, I think that's all for today. Mr. Yan will be in touch with Arden regarding the new tryouts."

Mom nodded and stood up. She hesitated for a moment and then turned toward Marni's parents. "Thank you. I'm sure this is difficult for you."

"We're very sorry," Mrs. Olsen said, sounding guilty and then looking at me with a sad face. "It won't happen again. And good luck with the Science Bowl."

I nodded, wondering how Marni could be so mean when her mom was so nice. She hadn't said very much other than her forced apology, which I didn't think was even a little sincere. I needed to know if she really was going to leave me alone. I needed to know if I still had reason to be afraid.

As I glanced over at her, she looked up at me. But as we locked eyes for that tiny second in time, she looked at me in a way I'd never seen before. Not anger or mockery, but something else completely, which I'd never have expected. Guilt.

"Let's go, Arden," Mom said as she moved toward the door. "I need to get dinner on."

And just like that, all the Marni drama was over.

TWENTY-TWO

As we pulled out of the school parking lot, I could tell by her slumped shoulders that Mom was exhausted. I felt bad—at least some of her tiredness was because she'd had to deal with me and my Meanie Marni drama. As for the rest, well, she did work a lot. And I couldn't remember the last time she'd done anything fun with her friends. Or gone on a date.

"How about we grab pizza?" I suggested. "Chloe's at dance tonight, but I'm sure Brandon would be into it."

She shook her head. "I took chicken out of the freezer."

"Put it in the slow cooker tomorrow," I suggested.

"You really are my smartest kid," she said and then winked. "Don't tell the others."

I smiled, even though I knew she was joking. "I'll order when we get home."

Her voice was a little trembly when she said, "Thank you, Arden."

"It's okay. I mean, it's not like eating pizza is a hardship."

She snorted and glanced over. "So you'd better tell me about Ludwig and how he was able to solve the mystery of the Science Bowl. There's something going on with him, isn't there? Birds aren't normally that smart, are they? What has my brother done?"

I wasn't sure how much I should tell her before I spoke with Uncle Eli. Not that I'd heard from him. But she was waiting, and I realized I couldn't keep it a secret from her. I didn't *want* to keep it from her.

I told her everything.

By the time I was finished, we were already parked in the underground garage in our building. Mom had taken the keys out of the car and was sitting still, facing me, with her mouth open in shock.

Finally she closed it, her teeth coming together with a click. "Math equations," she said again. "He can read. And do math equations."

I nodded. Again.

"So when he mimicked Marni…"

"I think he did it on purpose because he knew what she'd done was wrong and had hurt me."

She shook her head. "Arden, do you understand what this means? It means he can read, can perform tasks using critical thinking and higher reasoning. He knows right from wrong, he's…"

"Smart," I said when she struggled for the word. "*Super* smart."

"More than smart," she said, her eyes wide. "*Sentient*."

"What does *sentient* mean?" I asked.

"It means he can feel and perceive things. He's more than a problem-solver, although he's that too."

It sounded right. Ludwig was all those things and more.

She dropped her keys into her purse and opened the car door. "Come on. We really need to track down your uncle."

We did finally manage to get hold of Uncle Eli, but not until later that night, after Mom had sent him another email and a text, telling him it was not an emergency but we needed to talk to him very soon.

At nine o'clock, I was brushing my teeth for bed when the phone rang. I knew it was him. I spit out the toothpaste and tore out of the bathroom, yelling, "I'll get it!"

Of course, Mom beat me to it, giving me an amused look when I found her in the den, the phone to her ear. "We're all great," she said. "It's about Ludwig…no, he's fine. It's…you know what? I'll let Arden tell you. I'm putting you on speaker."

She pressed the button and put the phone down on the coffee table as I came into the room. I sat down beside her on the couch and leaned forward toward the phone. "Hi, Uncle Eli!" I was so excited to talk to him that I got teary.

"Hiya, Arden," he said, and his voice was so clear, it was hard to believe he was halfway around the world. And that it would be months before I'd see him again. Thinking about it brought more tears to my eyes.

Mom tilted her head at me, her eyebrows coming down into a concerned frown. "You okay?" she asked.

I nodded. "I miss you, Uncle Eli," I said.

Mom nodded, her frown turning to a sad smile. She missed him too.

"Same here, Arden," Uncle Eli said. He sounded tired. I'd googled time zones, and Guinea's was four hours ahead of ours, which meant he was up very late. "Tell me what's going on."

I took a deep breath and told him the same stuff I'd told my mom earlier in the car.

Once I was done there was only silence.

"You there, Eli?" Mom asked.

"Yeah, I'm here, I'm just..."

"I'm not making it up," I said, suddenly worried he'd think I was.

"I know, I know," he said quickly, and I could hear the excitement in his voice. "It's just a lot to take in. When I left, he...wow, this is new. So you're giving him the daily vitamins..."

"Yes," I said. "Fresh food and water every day, and a tablespoon of his vitamin powder mixed in with his pellets."

There was a long pause. Long enough that I almost asked if he was still there. "You mean a *tea*spoon of powder," Uncle Eli said.

"Um, no, a *table*spoon—" It occurred to me in that second that I'd messed up. "Oh no! I must have used the wrong measuring spoon!"

Mom's eyes were wide.

"I'm so sorry, Uncle Eli! I hope I haven't—"

"It's okay, Arden," my uncle said with a chuckle. "It won't hurt him. But...okay, so confession time?"

Confession time? Mom and I both leaned closer to the phone, eager to hear what he was going to say.

"The *actual* reason I'm here in Africa? I'm doing research on an old local legend about smart birds that come from this area. *Really* smart birds that villagers say can reason and think like humans."

"Birds that are sentient!" I said, beaming a smile at Mom.

"Exactly!" Uncle Eli exclaimed, obviously impressed. "Anyway, the legend is that they are reincarnated loved ones. The souls of family members who have passed on find their way into the rainforest and attach themselves to parrot eggs. When the birds hatch, it's like the loved ones have been reborn."

"Or re*hatched*," I said, but then what he was saying sunk in. "Whoa, so they're, like, ghosts trapped inside birds? That's so weird." And kind of scary.

"So the legend says," Uncle Eli went on. "The locals like the legend because it means their loved ones are close and can fly and live the life of a bird—they don't really think of them as ghosts. It's just part of their folklore."

"It's a lovely legend," Mom said, nodding. "But you can't tell me *you* believe that's what's going on."

Not my uncle, the science nerd who questioned everything. Who'd taught *me* to question everything.

He laughed. "It *is* a lovely legend. And I sort of wish it was true. But you know me very well, Claire. I had to get to the bottom of the science."

"Twin brains," I said. Mom nudged me with her arm, but she was smiling.

"Heh," Uncle Eli said. "Anyway, a few locals have speculated that what makes the birds different here is the bark of a tree that is only found in this one grove. It's very rare and has never been identified anywhere else in the world. The local birds like it and gnaw on the bark, sharpening their beaks and ingesting some of it."

"So how does that—oh, wait! The vitamin powder!" I said as it all clicked into place.

"The vitamin powder," Uncle Eli confirmed. "It's ground bark. I commissioned a local trail guide to send me some, but either it's lost its potency over time, or it wasn't as pure as I thought because the small dose—one teaspoon—should have worked. But when it didn't, I started to doubt the theories and came here to study them for myself."

"Wait a minute. My mistake made it work!" I said, bouncing a little because I'd helped! I'd made Ludwig smart! I looked at Mom. She smiled at me, and I could tell she was proud.

"A lot of great science happens by accident," Uncle Eli said. "Insulin, penicillin, quinine—some of the world's most important medicines—were discovered through accidents or mistakes that happened during research."

"Whoa, really?" I said, but it made sense. That's what research and employing the scientific method was all about.

"Sure. I mean, you have to be careful with the science that's dangerous, like Marie Curie found out with plutonium, when she—"

"Back on track, Eli," Mom said in a dry tone, making me laugh.

"Right," my uncle said. "Anyway, you've helped me prove it's the bark that makes these birds special. I…this is amazing. I wish I could come home."

My heart fell into my gut. "Why can't you?" I asked. "If you know what it is now?"

"I still need to study here for a few months, if not the full term of my sabbatical," he said. "The local birds are my research—Ludwig was something of my own experiment. One that I admittedly didn't really expect to work."

"But it did, so…" I felt my throat close up on my words. I missed him so much, especially now.

"I can't, Arden," he said, regret in his voice. "But I'm going to need you to fulfill a very important role now. I need you to act as my research assistant with Ludwig. I need you to keep detailed journals of what he's done that's remarkable, starting from the first time you gave him the increased measure of the bark powder."

"Really?" I said. "You want me to help with your research?"

"Of course! You're the one who made it happen. Assuming you want to."

I looked to my mom to ask if it was okay, and she just shrugged like it was up to me.

"Of course I do!" I said. "I'll be the best research assistant ever!"

"I know you will," he said, and I could hear the real pride in his voice. Then he yawned loudly. "I need to hit the hay, but I promise to be in touch more. Getting settled has taken a lot out of me, but it'll get better once I'm a few days into my routine. You have a good night, Arden. Let me talk to your mom, okay?"

"Sure, Uncle Eli. Thanks."

Mom picked up the phone and turned off the speaker. I left the den and went into the dining room. It was dark, and I didn't want to turn on the light to disturb Ludwig too much. I could still see him up on his branch perch, his eyes on me. "I just talked to Uncle Eli," I whispered to him. "He says hi and wants me to be his research assistant. Isn't that the coolest?"

"Happy dance!" Ludwig exclaimed as he started bobbing up and down. I laughed and joined him, the two of us dancing together even though there was no music.

"All right," I said a little breathlessly after a few minutes. "Time for bed. Good night, Ludwig."

He fluffed up his feathers and settled on his perch, one foot lifting and disappearing into his feathers as he prepared for sleep.

As I left the dining room, I heard him say in his little birdy voice, "Sleep tight, Arden."

I smiled. Yeah, Ludwig was way cooler than a Labradoodle.

EPILOGUE

Regional Science Bowl Finals

We were tied. There was one question left, which would determine the winners of the Regional Science Bowl. We had won the citywide competition, and now we were here, competing for the grand prize—an entire week for our team at STEM camp.

I was so nervous. My heart was pounding, my brain was firing, and I really had to pee, but none of that mattered.

All that mattered was this one final question. My hand hovered over the buzzer. I was ready. I looked over at Cabbage, and he nodded at me. He was ready too.

Brian and Charlotte were on the other side of him, and they each caught my eye and nodded.

It was go time.

The team on the other side of the stage was good, but we were better—between the four of us, we knew almost everything.

The quizmaster up at the podium cleared his throat. "All right," he said into the microphone, making my heart thump even harder and faster.

This is it.

"For the tie-breaker," the man said, his words coming out of his mouth so slowly that I wanted to yell at him to hurry up. "In terms of taxonomy, or biological classification, macaws, cockatoos and lorikeets belong to what order?"

I slammed my hand down on the buzzer so hard it almost slid off the table.

"Arden?" the man said, recognizing my buzz-in.

Unable to contain myself, I yelled out, "Psittaciformes!"

The man looked down at his index card and then smiled at me. "Correct!"

Right, like I wouldn't know *that* answer!

The four of us jumped up and embraced in a group hug. A second later Cabbage and Brian pulled back and high-fived each other.

"We're going to STEM camp and Nationals!" Charlotte said into my ear as we hugged and jumped up and down. "You did it, Arden!"

"*We* did it," I said. "All of us."

I looked out into the audience, wishing hard that Uncle Eli could have been out there. But he'd be excited to get my email when I told him how we'd won and what the final question was.

Mom was there with Simon, because of course they were dating now and were, if I may say so, an absolutely adorable couple. They were on their feet, applauding harder than anyone (except for maybe Mrs. Devi, who was standing on the other side of Mom).

Mom was smiling and wiping at her eyes, because sometimes when she was really proud, she got teary. I had to turn away or I was going to get teary too.

"That was amazing, Arden," Cabbage said beside me. "All that studying paid off."

"It was a bird question! How ridiculous is that?"

"I know," he said. "It was meant to be."

I poked myself in the temple. "Good thing I have a bird brain."

Cabbage grinned. "With what we know, that's hardly an insult."

"I know!" I laughed. "And speaking of birds, Ludwig's going to *love* hearing about this. Too bad we couldn't bring him to watch. But we'll tell him all about it later, and we'll celebrate with a giant dance party."

"Count me in," Cabbage said, doing a floss-dance move and making me giggle. Then I noticed Mr. Yan waving us over to the side of the gym.

"Come on, guys," I said, putting one arm around Cabbage's shoulders and the other around Charlotte's as I smiled at Brian. "Let's go get our trophy."

NOTE: FACT VS. FICTION*

*Warning: If you haven't read the book yet, there are spoilers below!

This book is a work of fiction—but it is a fact that, as of writing this note, I have had Gabby, a Timneh African Grey parrot, in my life for over twenty-one years. That's right, I've raised a bird to be old enough to vote and drive and go off to college, but she's given no indication that she wants to leave the nest (yes, I went there).

Birds are fun pets, but they are very messy, can be loud, have challenging and strong personalities and can live for a very long time. So before you ask your family to add a parrot to your holiday wish list, please do your research. If you do have your heart set on a pet bird and get the okay, I would strongly suggest you start out small. Budgerigars (budgies) and cockatiels are small, sweet and friendly birds, and they can even learn to talk a little.

Still, be like Arden and do your research.

I first got the idea for this book back in 2015, when I was cleaning Gabby's cage and setting out new grocery flyers in the bottom tray. I thought it would be funny if she could actually read them and understand what they said. What would happen then?

Boom! Book idea (as often happens—ideas are literally everywhere).

Anyway, while this book was inspired by my Gabby, and much of Ludwig's personality was based on hers (and how I imagine she would act if she were even smarter than she is), I also took a lot of liberties.

The tree bark that made Ludwig smart in the book isn't real. I totally made that up. Also, while birds can be trained to do some really intelligent things, such as identifying colors, objects and symbols; very basic counting and doing simple math; and answering thoughtful questions about things in their world, it's very unlikely they'd ever learn enough to be able to read and understand what they're reading.

We often take for granted that symbols on a page (like the ones you're looking at right now!) can represent abstract ideas, items and even conversations. Using language is complex enough, but reading and using symbol patterns the way we do requires processing by a very advanced brain. The kind of brain that most living creatures don't have. Dolphins, some great apes and, yes, African Grey parrots are known to be the thinkers of the animal world, but none can quite hold a candle to human intelligence.

That said, there are so many cool things about parrots that *are* true, and they are very smart, communicative creatures.

African Greys originate from, you guessed it, Africa, but many are bred for pets in North America. I did my research and found a reputable breeder in my area and reserved Gabby from the time she was an egg, similar to how many people reserve puppies from dog breeders. When she was a baby, the breeder put a permanent ring on Gabby's foot with her breeder information and hatch date on it (just like Ludwig's).

Gabby's wings are clipped for the same reasons that Ludwig's were—safety. She is a great climber and comes out of her cage every day for a bit of outside time. She loves peanuts and apples and tearing toys apart with her small but strong beak.

Gabby talks and makes a lot of noises that she learned from the world around her—our home. She often vocalizes in a way that is contextually correct—in other words, she pays attention and makes sounds that fit the situation. For example, even from a different room, she can hear me open and close the microwave, and when I reach to push the buttons, she beats me to it and beeps, sounding exactly like the appliance. When the TV is on and we laugh, she often laughs along (in my voice). Sometimes, if we're watching a sit-com, she'll laugh along with the show's laugh track even if the humans in the room aren't laughing.

She calls the cat when it's his dinnertime and asks the dog if she needs to go out when we go near the back door. She makes the same noise when she yawns as I do, which tells me she recognizes what a yawn is, which was one of my first clues that she really does pay attention to our behavior.

The way Ludwig watched Arden in the book is how Gabby watches us. You may not know what the bird is thinking, but there's clearly intelligence there. You just know they're paying attention.

Obviously, I'm not the only person who has figured out that birds are smart. Greys have long been known to be extremely intelligent, and the research by Dr. Irene Pepperberg that I mentioned in this book is absolutely real. Alex was a real bird and research subject, and you can learn more about Dr. Pepperberg's work, birds and studies at the Alex Foundation website (alexfoundation.org).

Finally, I've put together a page on my website where I'll also post some videos and resources. Check it out at joannelevy.com/BirdBrain.

ACKNOWLEDGMENTS

Beware: Bird puns ahead.

While I know my parrot, Gabby, would like to demand *all* the credit, it takes a flock to make a book and get it to market, so again, here I am thanking all those who had a hand (wing?) in this one.

Thank you to Lena Coakley, who gave me excellent justification for naming a character Cabbage when the idea popped into my head back in 2016. Also, thank you to Denise Mitchell for help with plotting back then. I'll be honest and say I have no recollection of what Denise helped me with, but it's in my notes, so it happened and I'm sure it was something important.

Gina Rosati and Terry Lynn Johnson, thank you so much for reading early drafts and offering up comments and suggestions. Your encouragement kept me going and convinced me that this book would sell one day.

A big thank-you happy dance to Tanya Trafford, who first read this book way back when and then officially acquired it for Orca before she flew the coop to pursue other exciting adventures. This was the sixth book of mine that Tanya brought into the pod, and I am eternally grateful for, and proud of, all the great work we did together.

Thank you to Sarah Howden, who took this project under her wing and worked with me to polish it up and take it from an ugly duckling to the beautiful swan you hold in your hands. We were very much in sync from the beginning, and I so appreciate her excellent vision, perspective and hard work.

Huge thanks to Andrew and Ruth for the ongoing support and making me feel like a welcome member of the Orca flock.

To Rachel, the cover designer, thank you again for doing such an amazing job and making this book look like a fun and exciting read that every kid will love. That front cover! And the back cover, with all the details, is absolute perfection! And a big high four (you know, because birds have four toes) to Amy Qi, who illustrated it and the bio pics for both me and Gabby so perfectly.

As always, thank you to the rest of the team who worked diligently behind the scenes to put this book together and get it out in the world: Kaedra and Mya, Susan, Sarah, Ella, Mark, Doeun and Vivian.

Much gratitude to Hilary McMahon for the ongoing support, encouragement, cheerleading, crowing and, you know, that necessary selling and contract stuff.

And last, but never, ever least, thanks to my own little flock, starting with the furred and feathered beings with whom I share my home. I am ever amused, comforted and humbled by your presence. I am a better human for having all of you in my life.

And, finally, the biggest thank-you of all to my husband, Deke, who is ever perched by my side. His enduring support keeps me going, and I will never take for granted his love, encouragement and willingness to listen to me talk out plots. Sir, you are forever the wind beneath my wings.

Joanne Levy is the award-winning author of a number of books for young people, including *Double Trouble*, *Fish Out of Water* and *The Book of Elsie* in the Orca Currents line and the middle-grade novels *The Sun Will Come Out*, *Small Medium at Large* and *Sorry For Your Loss*, which was nominated for the Governor General's Literary Award and won the Canadian Jewish Literature Award. She lives in Clinton, Ontario.

Gabby, avian consultant for this book, enjoys peanuts and apples, wood-working (particularly whittling), reading (actually, shredding) books, impersonating the microwave, dancing, yelling at her feline and canine co-conspirators and laughing at the television. While she has pooped on many papers, *Bird Brain* is her first professional collaboration.